# Serendipity

# Serendipity

Dear Sandra,

With Best Wishes,

*(signature)*

RASHMI KAIMAL

authorHOUSE®

*AuthorHouse*™
*1663 Liberty Drive*
*Bloomington, IN 47403*
*www.authorhouse.com*
*Phone: 1-800-839-8640*

*First published by AuthorHouse    02/03/2012*

*ISBN: 978-1-4678-8464-8 (sc)*
*ISBN: 978-1-4678-8465-5 (ebk)*

# Contents

*For Radhika and Renuka*

*With All My Love*

# Serendipity

"It really isn't that bad you know,"

Elizabeth gasped. She looked all around. There was nobody there. All she could hear was the gentle whistle of the breeze and the ripple of tiny waves in the stream below. It must have been her imagination.

"Seriously, don't look so worried . . ."

Now Elizabeth was on her feet! It *most definitely* was not her imagination this time! With wide eyes she looked down to where she thought the voice was coming from. Next to her bag sat the tiniest, most beautiful creature Liz had ever seen—*a pink-winged Fairy!* It smiled at her.

"Hi there, I'm Serendipity."

Elizabeth Atkins was speechless . . .

# The Sahara

*1*

It all began in September.

"You're up early, Liz," said Christine Atkins as her daughter pranced into the kitchen.

"I don't want to be late for the Coach, mum. It's going to be waiting at Chapel gate." Elizabeth fumbled with her shoe laces whilst her mother poured some milk onto her cornflakes.

"Uff, I wish I had shoes like Helena," she grumbled, referring to her younger sister's trainers with Velcro fasteners.

"Perhaps you'd like to go to year three like Helena as well," said her mum. "Elizabeth if you spent a little less time day-dreaming and a little more time concentrating on the task at hand you wouldn't have to do it ten times over!"

"I'm not daydreaming, mum. I'm just planning for the future, like you and dad. It's deep and serious thought!" Elizabeth smiled.

"Oh, is that so? Well, sweetheart, the difference is that thankfully, Dad and I stop *planning* and start *doing* things once in a while. Otherwise, we'd all be just sitting round the house daydreaming—oops, sorry—I mean *planning*, as you'd like to call it."

"All right mum, you win. I *am* trying you know. Ok I'd better get going now." Elizabeth gulped down the last bit of cereal and made her way to the door.

"Don't forget to tie your hair, Lizzy" yelled her mum as Elizabeth ran out.

"I will. Please give Helena a kiss from me and dad too. Bye"

In no time Elizabeth was out of the gate and running down the slope that led into the village pulling her shoulder length brown hair into a pony tail in the process.

It was the beginning of a new year at Primrose High, Elizabeth's school. Earlier on in the week, her class teacher, Ms Fitzgerald informed the class that the school had arranged an outing.

"This is just the beginning, girls", said Ms FitzGerald, "lots of hard work lies ahead and it's not easy getting back to the grind after a long, fun filled summer vacation. Your brains are usually still at the beach, lazing around, very reluctant to engage in anything constructive. So Ms Barrymore and I thought that it would be nice to welcome you in on a more enthusiastic note. We've arranged a trip to 'The Sahara' this Friday. Ms Barrymore and a couple of other teachers will be accompanying us and . . ."

Ms Fitzgerald tried to complete her sentence in vain as the class broke into rapturous applause at the prospect of going to the popular amusement park.

"Girls, please. This is a class room. Well, enthusiasm certainly doesn't seem to be low now, does it? Good grief! This is total cacophony! Now quieten down."

Immediately the sound mellowed into a few whispers and faint 'I can't waits'.

Ms Fitzgerald was one of the girls' favourite teachers. Although this was the first time she was their class teacher, Ms Fitzgerald had taught the girls English since year 1. With her crisp sense of humour and keen interest in every aspect of the girls' school life from their incorrect grammar to their constantly fluctuating fashion sense, the fifty three year old teacher had won a very special place in their hearts. Ms Fitzgerald was due to retire at the end of the year and her devoted students were already planning a memorable farewell. Now, Ms Fitzgerald had given them yet another reason to wish she wouldn't leave. 'The Sahara Yipee . . . ,'

Friday came sooner than expected. After a brisk ten minute walk Elizabeth was at Chapelgate Bus station where a large coach was parked. A few other girls were waiting nearby. They waved when they saw Elizabeth. One of them was Abigail Swift, Liz's best friend. Elizabeth and Abigail had known each other since they were in nursery. Now, ten years later they were in high school and still found nothing more pleasurable than sharing each other's dessert at lunchtime!

"Hey Liz, wonder what we're going to have for lunch. They have the best chicken salad at 'The Sahara' you know," said Abigail

"We're not even on the coach yet Abi and you're already thinking of food," teased Elizabeth

Ms Fitzgerald was speaking to the coach driver. She smiled at Elizabeth and motioned to the girls to board the coach. There was a minor kerfuffle, as the class negotiated 'terms and conditions' for occupancy of the window seat.

"Come on, girls! Stop behaving like two year olds. Kids in kindergarten have disagreements like this and they are a good few years younger than you lot."

Sitting next to Abigail, Elizabeth looked around her. Most of the faces were familiar. The majority of the girls in Liz's class had known each other since primary school, and were good friends. There were a few 'damsels' Elizabeth felt less inclined to mingle with. Alison Radcliffe was one of them. The Miss 'High and Mighty' of the class always made it a point to 'make her point'. Her father was a successful business man and Alison was used to the easy life. She incessantly spoke of how her parents had bought her the trendiest fashion accessories and outfits and taken her to an expensive resort for her last holiday. The list was endless. Alison had her own clique—Natasha, Chloe, Megan and Rebecca. They were thoroughly mesmerised by Alison's affluence and convinced that by being her 'best friend', some of Alison's glamour would rub off on them!

Other than these few aspiring 'celebrities,' the girls in Elizabeth's class were down to earth, sensible and caring. There was only one new girl, Mirabel Mitchell. Mirabel had previously studied at the Co-operative School in the neighbouring village. Her consistently high scores in science won Mirabel a scholarship to attend Primrose High. In spite of her notable achievements Mirabel was extremely shy. She hardly spoke a word unless spoken to but was very polite and always smiling. Mirabel seemed content just listening to the other girls' endless prattle at break time, her only contributions to the conversation being an occasional nod of the head.

Elizabeth nudged Abigail on the shoulder.

"Don't you think Mirabel is really sweet? I just wonder why she's so quiet. It's almost as though she's afraid to speak for fear of being laughed at."

"Oh Liz, you think too much. Yes, Mirabel is quiet. But just because some people don't banter on nineteen to the dozen like you do, it doesn't mean there's something wrong with them. Now stop analysing things and try and see if you can spot the 'Dune Dragon' before I can."

The Dune Dragon was the most talked about feature of 'The Sahara'. A Roller Coaster with more loops and slopes than any other in the region, the Dragon was everything its name suggested—terrifying! As the coach sped on, the backdrop of 'The Sahara' came into view. Even from a distance the park looked amazing! Ever since its opening a couple of years earlier,

'The Sahara' had won acclaim for its originality. Undoubtedly, the amusement park was exceptional in providing the 'thrill' factor. However, what made it unique was its landscape. 'The Sahara' was nothing short of a tropical paradise. That too, in the middle of a country which had only recently recorded one of its coldest winters in twenty years!

After an hour's drive, the coach pulled up at its destination. The gates of the 'The Sahara' loomed large; two iron edifices shaped and painted to look like enormous palm trees. The girls lined up at the entrance.

Ms Fitzgerald, Ms Taylor, Ms Roberts and Ms Barrymore stood nearby. One of the park's officials came up to Ms. Barrymore to give her the entry passes.

"Alright, girls'" said Ms Fitzgerald, "We'll be here the whole day and we'd like you to make the most of it. No ... that doesn't mean going on every ride at least 10 times!!!!!" The girls giggled.

"There is a lot more to see here than just bumper cars. And to make sure that you learn as much as you can, staff at 'The Sahara' has very kindly helped us in setting up something else—a treasure hunt."

A torrent of questions instantly headed Ms Fitzgerald's way.

"What treasure Ms Fitzgerald?"

"Do we get to keep it?" said another voice.

"Is this a trick?" yet another.

"Shush . . . quiet everyone. Unless you stop wittering on, we are not going to get past the entrance, let alone, find any treasure. Now listen carefully", continued Ms. Fitzgerald. You will be split into four groups, one teacher in charge of each group The so-called 'treasures' are just little knick knacks that Ms Barrymore and I picked up at '*Delayna's*', a token to welcome you to High School. We thought it would be the best way to get you to concentrate on the botanical aspects of the 'Sahara'. Most importantly, we want to prove that we 'oldies' aren't as out of fashion as you may think! Who knows, some of you may even find a '**MISschief**' memorabilia or two."

'**MISschief**' was the latest teenage pop sensation—every school girl's wannabe, and the girls found it extremely difficult to contain their excitement.

"We'll only begin the treasure hunt after lunch, so you have the next two hours to spend on the rides. After lunch, we'll move into 'The Garden'. The clues to the treasure hunt are quite simple, so long as you make an effort to learn as much as you can about each plant. Well, that's all I'm saying. Remember to stay in your group and inform your teacher if you need anything. Oh! Try to not to scream too loud while you're on those monstrosities. Gosh!!! I don't know how you can possibly find these rides pleasurable. Just the *thought* of plunging down the water flume makes me want to be sick!! Now, off you go, enjoy yourselves!" Ms. Fitzgerald stepped aside and the girls made their way into the 'Sahara's' fun park, 'The Danger zone'.

Screams and squeals plummeted into the fences surrounding the 'Danger Zone,' as Elizabeth and her mates enjoyed the rides. They were still wishing for more, when Ms Barrymore rounded them up for lunch, which was a sumptuous spread, compliments of 'The Sahara'. A lip smacking half an hour later, it was time for the treasure hunt.

# A Taste of the Exotic

THE GIRLS WALKED towards 'The Garden'.

"I actually love this part of 'The Sahara' with or without the treasure hunt, Abi" said Elizabeth. "It is a treasure in itself, don't you think, like going to a faraway land and finding shapes and colours that you've never even imagined."

'The Garden' was a vast expanse spread over six acres of land. It was divided into four zones—The Fruit Factory, Palms and Pines, Sand dunes, and 'The Kaleidoscope'. The Zones' temperature controlled environment housed many rare species. 'The Kaleidoscope', in keeping with its name, was a feast for the eyes with innumerable flowerbeds and trees in myriad of colours.

The girls decided to move through each section on their own taking care not to lose their group.

"Remember, the plants are your clues" said Ms Barrymore

First they ventured into the 'fruit factory'. A tempting ensemble of fruit trees welcomed the girls. Avocados, Lychee, Button Mango Steen, and Passion Fruit were but a few of the names that lined the walkway. Much to their disappointment large placards saying 'DO NOT TOUCH' *also* lined the walkway, forcing the class to dispel any hopes of helping themselves to a tasty bite or two.

"Hey look", someone shouted.

Elizabeth turned and saw that it was Dionne, one of the quieter members of Liz's class. Everyone went closer. Dionne was holding a small packet with *Delayana's* insignia, **'DY'**, clearly embossed.

"I found one", smiled Dionne.

Now standing next to her, the others read the label attached to the tree Dionne was pointing to. It said 'Theobroma Cacao—The Chocolate tree'

"I was looking at the description and then noticed something glistening on the branches. See for yourselves," Dionne moved aside so that the other girls could get nearer to the plant.

On closer observation the group saw that attached to the trees' leaves were little Cadburys chocolates! So **'that'** was the clue. The Cacoa plant should give Cocoa Beans. Not Chocolates!!!! The girls burst out laughing. It was not going to be that hard after all; the key was to read the information given about each plant, carefully. Most probably, hidden treasure would be lurking around plants which fit their descriptions *perfectly!*

The next hour was spent in the quest for hidden treasures. There were cheers and claps each time the hunt bore fruit. Primrose High was set to make history in the field of new scientific discoveries! Surely, Bottlebrush trees with actual bottle brushes, African Moons with small smiley faces shaped like moons, and Angel Wing Begonias with Christmas tree angels stuck to them would be a novelty for the most experienced botanist!! Abigail came running up to Elizabeth waving a bottle brush in one hand, clutching her precious loot in the other.

"I thought you found baby bottle brushes in Mothercare, not on exotic trees", she said bubbling with excitement at the thought of what she would find in her packet.

The excitement continued through each zone. Elizabeth was wonderstruck at the size of the trees in 'Palms and Pines'. Her eyes gazed up at a large pine called 'Bunya Bunya'. *What a funny name. Gosh! Could trees be this tall!* The Bunya Bunya dwarfed everything in its vicinity. Like Jack's beanstalk, it seemed to rise and disappear into the clouds.

Liz was so engrossed in gazing at the gigantic tree that she almost tripped over one of her shoe laces. As she bent over to tie them, she realised the rest of her group was quite a distance away. Should she wait?

"*I suppose they'll catch up,*" she thought, "*these trees are too interesting to stand around doing nothing*".

Liz managed to wave to Ms Barrymore, who signalled to her to carry on down the path.

"We'll catch up with you, Liz" she shouted. "Wait when you reach the entrance to the 'Dunes.'"

Funnily enough, in spite of all her attention to detail, Liz still hadn't found any treasure. Just as this began to dawn on her, something caught her eyes.

"Was that someone reading a newspaper?"

When Liz approached the conifer, her suspicions were confirmed. Indeed there was somebody leaning back against the tree trunk, holding a copy of the Daily Mail.

"Huh! How odd. Oh well! The surroundings are so peaceful maybe it's the best place to read the news or do a crossword puzzle. No harm in saying Hello, though."

"Hello there," she called out. No reply. The person whose face was hidden behind the newspaper was thoroughly absorbed in whatever the 'Daily Mail' had to offer. He or she didn't move a muscle even though Liz's footsteps and voice were clearly audible.

'Wow, some people really enjoy their crosswords, eh. Well, they could at least say hello!" Determined to elicit a response Liz moved closer. She almost screamed in horror! The arms and hands holding the newspaper were covered in **thick dark hair**!

Thankfully, Elizabeth's panic stricken movements made the newspaper fall, revealing a cheeky grin and equally mischievous eyes. Instead of screaming Liz's face lit up with a relieved smile when she saw that the owner of the long hairy arms was actually a monkey.! Not a real one, an almost life size stuffed toy.

"Phew, you almost frightened me to death", Liz told the monkey as she lifted him up. "Now, who do you belong to?

And why on earth did they leave you here with a newspaper? Hmmm, could this be a clue?"

Liz looked at the Pine again trying to find any details. The tree looked similar to the Bunya Bunya. "Ah there it is." Liz read the name on the label.

'**Monkey Puzzle Tree. *Araucaria Araucana*'**.

This *had* to be a clue. Elizabeth looked around. Were there any packets, any boxes, and any treasures? Nothing. She looked at the branches to see if she'd missed something there. Still nothing.

*'That's funny, this definitely is a clue. Yet I'm certain there's no hidden treasure here, apart from Mr Bananas!! Whoever planted the clue must have missed out the gift. Oh Well!! You win some, you lose some",* Liz sighed. She walked towards 'the Dunes', leaving Monkey Man to solve his puzzle.

"Oops! "Once again Liz tripped over almost hitting the ground with her nose.

"Hey! I just fastened my laces." Scrunching up her face, she stood up annoyed that her uniform trousers were no longer spotlessly clean. "These stupid laces! I'm definitely going to buy new . . . oh, what's this?"

Elizabeth saw that her laces weren't the culprits. She had tripped over something else, a rectangular box, lying next to her feet. Elizabeth looked at the box, it was nothing spectacular. She picked it up. The box wasn't very big, but it was long enough to use as a jewel box or pencil case. It had small multicoloured stones around the edges, and fine carvings on the sides. Liz was certain that her pretty find was the treasure that her monkey friend was pointing her to. The box must have been positioned in such a way that anyone would have tripped over it. Luckily for Elizabeth, she was the one who fell first!

Delighted, Liz waited for Abigail and the others to join her. She showed them the box.

"So you found your pot of gold, Liz," smiled Ms Barrymore. "That's pretty, isn't it? Hmm, I don't remember buying it at Delayna's. Oh yes!! It must be one of the items that Ms Fitzgerald said she would pick up from the gift shop opposite her home. That's probably why I can't remember seeing it. It certainly is dainty. Ok, come on girls we need to move on."

The outing was coming to an end. In another half an hour, the class would have to board the coach for their journey back home. The girls were waving around what they'd found-, purses, pencil cases, hair bands, MISschief emblazoned handkerchiefs. It was indeed an exuberant bunch of treasure hunters that spent the last half an hour of their visit, screaming as they pushed one another down the slopes of the Sahara's miniature sand dunes.

"Hey Abi, how about giving that cactus a hug when you reach the bottom?" yelled Liz sliding down one of the slopes holding on to Abigail.

"And all these years I thought you were my best friend, you wicked witch"

Soon the girls were lined up and Ms Fitzgerald did a headcount to make sure that no one was still digging for treasures inside the gates.

"Yes, all here. Little Bo Peep hasn't lost any sheep today. Jump aboard girls." For convenience, instead of going back to Chapelgate, the coach would take the girls to school so that they could return home as they normally do.

Eager to describe the day's happenings to their families, the girls sank into their seats, exhausted. Still, in spite of their aching limbs and droopy eyes tiny sparks of excitement continued to flicker, like smouldering ember waiting to be rekindled.

# A New Friend

THE LARGE COACH drove up to the main entrance and the girls trooped out making sure they had their precious 'treasure' with them.

"Would you please go straight to your classroom and wait till the bell rings before making your way out. I hope you've enjoyed the day, girls. Once again, welcome to high school." Ms Fitzgerald motioned to the girls to proceed into the school hall. "Bye girls and see you on Monday."

Before they got to the classroom Ms. Fitzgerald patted Elizabeth on the shoulder. "Liz, can I have a word with you please?"

"Yes, Ms Fitzgerald,"

Elizabeth followed her class teacher into her office.

"Now don't be alarmed. I haven't summoned you here to admonish you." Ms Fitzgerald sat down at her desk asking Elizabeth to sit down in the chair opposite.

"Elizabeth, although I've only been your class teacher for the past three days, I've known you for much longer, long enough to know that you are exceptionally talented and extremely intelligent." Ms FitzGerald reached out and patted Elizabeth's cheek before she continued to speak.

"I've also spent the same length of time wondering how someone so capable could possess an attention span that lasts no longer than the interval between two successive daydreams!"

Elizabeth grinned sheepishly.

"Elizabeth dear, this is just the beginning of the most crucial years in your school life. You need to be more focused. I wouldn't be telling you this unless I thought you could. We all know you have a gift, Elizabeth. What you have to realise is that *that* is exactly what it is, a 'gift'—something, which you have been blessed with. Now you have to keep your side of the bargain." Ms Fitzgerald paused for a moment. "Those earrings are very pretty Elizabeth, Gold?"

"Yes, Ms Fitzgerald. They actually belonged to my Grandmother."

"Umm, there's nothing like Gold to stand the test of time. Liz, I'm sure you know that Gold is one of the most expensive and sought after naturally occurring metals in the world."

Elizabeth nodded.

"Did you also know that Gold in its purest form, or 24 carat gold as it is referred to, is so soft that it would be next to impossible to use it for jewellery? It simply would not withstand prolonged use. To make gold suitable for wear and tear it's blended with other metals like copper or nickel. You see, sometimes even the most valuable commodities need a boost to reach their full potential."

Ms Fitzgerald noticed Elizabeth's rather bemused expression.

"My point is Elizabeth, having a talent is not enough, especially with *your* aspirations. Just like Copper and Nickel are such vital reinforcements for Gold, you will need a solid foundation in other subjects too, as boring as they may seem. Most Universities and Colleges insist on this. Am I making any sense, Elizabeth?"

"Yes, Ms Fitzgerald. It's just that I don't know how to . . . ," Elizabeth hesitated, searching for the right words.

"Well, you must *find out*, how to. We're all here to provide you as much support as you need, especially Ms Roberts." Ms Fitzgerald put her arm over Elizabeth's shoulder. "Liz, take things in the right spirit. You'll be alright as long as you do."

"I'll try my best. Thank you Ms Fitzgerald."

"You're most welcome, Elizabeth. Now run along and enjoy your weekend." Elizabeth turned towards the door.

"Elizabeth, there's something else I'd like to tell you."

"Yes Ms?"

"I personally know a girl who used to be one of the best daydreamers of her time. She's now an excellent school teacher!" Ms. Fitzgerald winked at Elizabeth and started looking through the papers on her desk.

Elizabeth walked out comforted by her class teacher's encouraging words, but slightly daunted by the hard work that lay ahead. The school corridor was a mad rush as kids raced outside already rejoicing at the thought of another weekend. There were plans to meet friends, go to the cinema and of course one or two conscientious children who wanted to spend time together to complete homework!

Abigail had saved a seat for Liz on the school bus. Elizabeth and Abigail went to and from school together. The school bus would drop them off at the village crossroads from where they would walk the rest of the way.

The two friends sat side by side as they'd done for so many years, gazing out at the beautiful country side. They were too tired to engage in any conversation. Not that it mattered. With one person's head resting on the other's shoulder, there was no need for any words. Abigail and Elizabeth were true friends.

Abi's house was closer to the village than Liz's. The two friends hugged one another and agreed to meet up some time during the weekend.

"Maybe we can do our Maths homework together, Liz".

"Yeah, maybe, I'll call you. Bye Abi"

Flinging her bag over her shoulders, Liz continued walking. Her mind couldn't help ponder over Ms Fitzgerald's words. Unexpectedly, Elizabeth got low grades in the previous year's Maths assessments. It was unexpected because her marks in every other subject were far above average. According to her maths teacher, Ms Roberts, Elizabeth's low marks were more to do with her dislike of the subject rather than an inability to deal with numbers. Elizabeth was clever but careless! She knew she should pull herself together. If only she could find the motivation to put in the effort. But she hated Maths.

Elizabeth approached a small stream that flowed through the valley. Her house was just a few minutes away so she decided to sit down for a little while. As she continued to mull over Ms. Fitzgerald's words, Elizabeth took out a pencil and sketchpad from her bag. While her thoughts wandered around the day's events, her pencil took another path—fine lines, dark shadows, and pale reflections. In the moments that Elizabeth's mind grappled with her unending struggle with mathematics, her hand effortlessly created something quite exquisite—a beautiful impression of 'The Garden' at The Sahara with the Dune Dragon looming in the background. The thirteen year old clearly had a rare gift.

As she gave the picture some finishing touches, Liz glanced at her watch and suddenly realised she'd been sitting down for more than half an hour. With a deep sigh, she put her sketch pad back into her rucksack.

"It really isn't that bad you know,"

Elizabeth gasped. She looked all around. There was nobody there. All she could hear was the gentle whistle of the breeze, and the ripple of tiny waves in the stream below. It must have been her imagination.

"Seriously, don't look so worried . . . ,"

Now Elizabeth was on her feet! It *most definitely was not* her imagination this time! With wide eyes she looked down to where she thought the voice was coming from. Next to her bag sat the tiniest, most beautiful creature Liz had ever seen—*a pink-winged Fairy!* It smiled at her.

"Hi there, I'm Serendipity".

Elizabeth Atkins was speechless. Unable to even breathe, she sat transfixed as the fairy fluttered on to her bag.

"You can call me 'Tippy' if you like."

'Huh . . . What . . . Who are you? Oh God I must be dreaming. What's wrong with me?' Liz closed her eyes and started shaking her head vigorously. She must be more exhausted than she thought.

"You're going to make a fine mess of your brain if you shake your head like that".

Elizabeth closed her eyes for a few moments. When she reopened them, the fairy was still there. Still only half trusting her eyes, Elizabeth brought her face closer to the tiny creature hoping that proximity would somehow make her stop hallucinating. It didn't. It wasn't a hallucination.

Elizabeth's heart was pounding but she managed to find her voice.

"You really *are* here!? I can't believe this." Elizabeth stretched her arm out to see whether she could touch the fairy and gasped as she felt the feathery softness against her fingertips. The fairy smiled.

"You needn't be scared, Elizabeth, I am not going to eat you. Fairies are far gentler than that."

Elizabeth still couldn't say a word. This was so unbelievable.

"I am sure you've got lots of questions. Fire away".

"Yes . . . Umm, for starters who are you? Why are you here? Where do you come from?"—Is this really happening . . . Oh Gosh . . ."

"Hey Hey Hey, slow down, slow down, I heard you. Relax. I told you. I'm a friend."

"Well, my friends usually don't have wings."

"Who said I'm the 'usual' variety?"

"Fine, what 'variety' are you then? Please, please, please can you just answer my questions?"

Elizabeth was getting more perplexed with each passing moment.

"Oh alright, I'm a fairy. Surely, you guessed that much. Like I said before, you can call me Tippy. Now, remember that handsome monkey you met at the Sahara. That's my dad!"

"Your dad's a monkey?!"

"No, No, No silly . . . My dad came *disguised* as a toy monkey to make sure that I got into the right hands. His name is Gloryon, the King of fairies and my mum, Eleganta, is the Queen."

"This is getting more and more unbelievable," Elizabeth was beginning to feel slightly dizzy.

"You asked the questions, Elizabeth. These are the answers, believable or not."

"So why are you here now?"

"I was coming to that if you would just stop interrupting." The tiny fairy's even tinier face frowned at Elizabeth.

"Well, I'm not entirely sure why I'm here. I guess we'll just have to wait and see. My Dad seems to think you can help me get used to Diddy. But I don't agree . . ."

"Who's Diddy?" Elizabeth interrupted again.

"I don't want to talk about him."

"Well then how am I supposed to help you if you don't tell me who on earth Diddy is!!?"

"I don't know."

Elizabeth gave up. This could not be happening. She was speaking to a fairy! She sat on a moss covered stone, still dazed. The little creature flew down next to her.

"By the way, my Dad thinks I can help *you* too."

"Me? Why, for what?"

"I don't know *that* either!"

By now Elizabeth was exasperated.

"Great. That's very enlightening. Basically all you know is your name."

Serendipity flew onto Elizabeth's knee.

"Oh, so you've got all the answers have you? Tell me Miss 'Know It All', why are *you* sitting here throwing stones into the water feeling sorry for yourself, when you could be at home, drinking a lovely cup of hot chocolate?"

"Oh! That's because, uh, actually I just . . ."

"Exactly, we both don't know why we found each other. Whatever the reasons, they can't be that bad. Believe me; usually fairies are considered good luck charms of the *deluxe* category."

Elizabeth smiled. She touched Serendipity's wings to convince herself, once more, that she wasn't asleep.

"By the way", continued the fairy, "nobody should know about me except your parents and sister and they have to keep me a secret too. If not, I'll have to return home and my father will never give me a chance to come back. Now that's not going to be of much help to either of us, is it? Please promise me."

"Of course, I promise. I'm still shocked. I have to keep pinching myself to make sure you're real."

"Pinch all you want, darling. I'm not going anywhere anytime soon. So how about you take me home now, I'm kind of hungry."

Serendipity flew on to Liz's shoulder and gave her a quick kiss on the cheek. Coming from such tiny lips, Elizabeth felt as though, she had been tickled with a feather. Seeing the twinkle in Tippy's eyes, she started to giggle.

"Yes, you definitely *are* real and I think we're going to have a great time together. Imagine that. I thought I hadn't won anything at the Sahara. It turns out I found the most enchanting gift of all. You may not be a 'MISschief' keepsake. But I suspect you're going to be enough mischief for me. Tippy, what did you say your full name is?"

"Serendipity"

Elizabeth watched as the fairy flapped her delicate wings, spreading sparkly powder into the air.

"What a pretty name. Does it mean anything?"

Serendipity brought her face close to Elizabeth's ears.

"Yes, it does Elizabeth," she whispered. "It means to discover something very lucky by accident."

"Wow!" Elizabeth was spellbound yet again.

They crossed a bridge which took them over the shallow stream and up to a wooden gate. The gate had a stone plaque with the words *The Kohwai* engraved on it. Liz unlocked the gate.

"Welcome to my home Tippy" she said.

# *The Kohwai*

ELIZABETH LIVED IN the picturesque town of Matlock in the Peak District. The Kowhai, was a black and white cottage built in the early 1900s. It belonged to Liz's grandfather, who was a University Professor with a passion to learn about other countries and cultures. Sometimes he would sail for months to collect new information about other countries to share with his students and people who, like him, yearned to learn more about regions of the world still unfamiliar to them.

One such voyage, his most memorable, was his trip to New Zealand. A journey he shared with his new wife, shortly after their wedding. On their return from New Zealand, Elizabeth's grandparents decided to settle down in Matlock. They bought their first house and named it 'The Kohwai'—the national tree of New Zealand.

Prof. Atkins died soon after his son Richard, Elizabeth's father, graduated from Medical School. The Kowhai was now Richard Atkins's responsibility. He set up a practice in the village and soon gained popularity as the young doctor who always put his patients first. It was during this time that Dr Atkins met Liz's mother Christine, a kindergarten teacher, in the village school. They were soon married and Elizabeth was born two years later.

Elizabeth was not the only new addition to the family. One evening Dr Atkins came home with a companion for Elizabeth, a four month old

St Bernard puppy. They called him Bartholomew.

"Distinguished, eh, Chris," remarked Dr Atkins to his wife, extremely pleased with his choice of name.

"A tad too distinguished, I think. It's a mouthful in itself, Richard. Elizabeth can't even say 'mum' yet."

"She'll grow into it," said Dr Atkins, determined to have his way.

"Fine, we'll call him Bartholomew, but Toby for short" conceded Liz's mother.

And so Bartholomew Atkins became the most distinguished occupant of the Kowhai household, the Lord of the Manor!!

As Elizabeth and Serendipity approached the Kowhai, Tippy got her first glimpse of Liz's family. She saw the large photograph on the top of the fire place, a picture of Elizabeth's grandparents, under the Kowhai Tree on their honeymoon. Inside, Liz's sister Helena was laying the table.

"Mum, this is Liz's job. Why do I have to do it? Liz always gets away without having to do the housework."

Elizabeth's eight year old sister had been sulking ever since she discovered that she would not be accompanying Liz to The Sahara. Elizabeth's parents rolled their eyes. They were used to the usual 'complaints', every time one of their girls struggled to cope with the 'tragic brutality' of not being able to enjoy the same things—either by age, house rules or simply by sheer accident.

"Daddy, how come Helena gets to go with you and mum, I wish I didn't have these silly sums to do."

"Lizzy, that's my dress"

"No, it's not,"

"Yes, it is".

"It used to be mine',

"It isn't now",

"Fine"

"Why can't I stay up late, mum? Lizzy gets to"

"Helena, I promise I did not eat your biscuit, Bartholomew did."

A million and one exchanges in the eight years since Helena arrived. But with every single squabble, one thing was certain. Elizabeth and Helena were the best of friends and treasured each other's company more than anything. Some nights Elizabeth's parents would go to the girls' room, wondering why the bedroom lights were still on. They would find their girls fast asleep, arms around one another.

Tonight, though, Helena was feeling very sorry for herself and continued to grumble.

"It's not fair".

"Helena, please put those plates on the table and stop being melodramatic. You know that this was a school trip and you know there will be plenty of other occasions to go to the Sahara," said Liz's mother.

Helena still frowning carried the plates to the dining table, almost tripping over Bartholomew in the process.

"Toby, must you stick yourself right in the middle of the room?"

"Helena, that's enough now. Not another word."—Helena was really getting on Dr Atkins's nerves

It was almost six pm when Elizabeth rang the door bell, totally at a loss as to how to introduce her new friend to her family.

When Dr Atkins opened the door, he was taken aback at Liz's perplexed expression.

"Hello Liz, is everything ok darling?'

He gave her a hug as she walked in. "You look off colour; didn't you have a good time?"

"Oh no, Dad! I mean, yes, I had a great time. And, no, there's nothing wrong. I'm fine."

"You're probably just tired sweetheart. Now come on lets all have some tea. It's your favourite, Fish Pie."

"It's my favourite too mum," said Helena. She was intent on making her 'comeback' and getting into her parents' good books.

"I know, Lenny. But you've been such a sourpuss the whole afternoon I'm not even sure I want to speak to you."

"I'm sorry, mum. I know I've been a bit annoying."

"A *bit?* Darling you've been absolutely infuriating!" Dr Atkin's tone was calm yet stern.

"The last thing you want to see when you come home from work is a sulking, ungrateful child. You better learn to be more considerate Helena; it's not always about you. Do you understand?"

"Yes daddy. I'm sorry,"

Helena sat down quietly.

"Lets hear about your day, Lizzy," Mrs Atkins served out the pie. "Was it better than you expected?"

Elizabeth began to fumble with her fork and knife, unsure how to begin her 'fairy tale'. "Uh, it was nothing like I expected, mum."

She went silent again and began to cut out a piece of her pie. Elizabeth's thoughts were all over the place. The silence was interrupted when Toby barked. Where was Tippy? Suddenly she remembered.

"Toby, stop sniffing my bag, there's nothing in it for you. Stop it. Come here and have some pie if you want."

Inside the half open bag, Tippy was hiding behind Liz's pencil case, traumatised by the big dog's eyes peering down inquisitively. Toby's bark made her cower down even more. Serendipity was sure she was going to be struck down by

Bartholomew's doggie biscuit fuelled, curiosity charged missile of a snout any moment! The bag moved. This was it! She was doomed to be crushed by a four legged beast! Serendipity closed her eyes. Please let it be over quickly. Then she heard a voice.

"That's a good boy. Is that tasty? Good."

Serendipity opened her eyes expecting to feel excruciating pain. She felt nothing. Who was speaking? It was a woman's voice. Was God a lady!?

"Thanks mum. Toby just *eat* that pie and stay away from my bag."

"Elizabeth, why are you getting so high strung about the bag. Anyway you've rescued it now so please eat your dinner."

Elizabeth was looking inside the bag to make sure its 'items' were still safe. Tippy looked up at her, a little less confused and a lot more certain that the voice she had heard in her moment of peril belonged to Liz's mother, not God!

"Yes, I will, in a moment." Elizabeth continued to look into the bag attempting to make eye contact with Tippy. She managed to put her hand into the bag and touch Tippy very gently, reassuring her.

"Elizabeth, what *is* it with you and that bag?? Have you smuggled in a snake or something from the Sahara?"

"Well, it's not exactly a snake, Uh . . ."

"Elizabeth, I was just kidding. I know there are no snakes in the 'Sahara'! I'm just trying to wake you up. You're not yourself sweetheart. You're very distracted",

"She's just tired Christine. Lizzy, come on now. Finish off that pie and you can have an early night."

Dr Atkins reached out to move Elizabeth's bag onto an adjacent shelf. Elizabeth panicked.

"No!!! Wait, Dad."

"Lizzy, what's wrong with you?! This has gone on long enough. *What is in that bag!!?*"

Elizabeth could feel her pulse racing. She looked at her parents and Helena. She had to say something.

"The thing is, mum, it's rather unusual. I don't know quite how to begin. You see, we played this game at the Sahara, a treasure hunt."

"Well, you did go there to have fun," said Mrs Atkins, "what's so unusual about playing a game? So is *that* what you've got in your satchel, your treasure."

"Oooh, what is it Liz? Can I play with it too?" Helena couldn't contain her curiosity as her mind toyed with endless possibilities as to what the mystery item could be.

"There is no 'it', Helena. I didn't win anything."

"That's alright Liz, surely you know it doesn't matter. But what's in the bag then?"

"It's sort of hard to explain. I made a new friend,"

"That's nice, darling. Elizabeth, you are still not making much sense. Why should that be so hard to explain? And what has that got to do with your bag?" said Dr Atkins.

"She's a fairy, Dad."

Helena started to giggle. "Gosh, Sis! You really are tired."

"Quieten down Helena. Lizzy, would you like to have something to drink, love? You've had a long day."

"She's fine Mrs. Atkins. Just wants you to listen".

Tippy had flown out of the bag and was now sitting on top of the showcase.

"What was that? Richard, did you hear something?"

"It's *her* mum. I told you. Come here Tippy. Serendipity flew on to Liz's hand as her mum, dad and sister looked on in wide eyed amazement.

Helena felt as if her eyes would pop out of her head as she stared at the creature without even a blink.

"I'd like to introduce you to my new friend, Serendipity."

For the next couple of hours, Dr Richard Atkins, a man of science, listened and watched as everything around him began to defy any scientific explanation. Elizabeth described the day's events in detail. The treasure hunt was, of course, meant to be a year nine biology lesson in disguise. Elizabeth vividly recounted how her quest through The Sahara's manmade jungle had culminated in a monkey, a wooden box and a fairy!

Even Toby was mesmerised by this new creature. Now that he had actually seen the 'thing' that was hidden in Liz's bag, Bartholomew seemed rather uncertain how to approach it. There he was, as usual, plonked on his favourite rug. What was *not* usual was that for a change Toby wasn't half asleep! He sensed the excitement, and the sense of excitement that he sensed, was anything but ordinary. He, Bartholomew Atkins, would not let this most momentous event of extraordinariness go unmarked. As the most important member of the family it was his duty! Toby's doggy eyes and ears battled his doggy laziness to watch Tippy's every move.

When the clock struck midnight, Elizabeth half expected to wake up and realise that the spell was broken. That maybe Cinderella would run past in a frenzy, with a bunch of mice dressed like footmen, apologizing for the confusion! But nothing happened. No magic spell and no Fairy Godmother. But there certainly was a fairy.

"Unbelievable?" said Dr Atkins lifting Tippy towards him. "She's real Christine. Come here, Helena. I don't think there is anything to be frightened about."

"Yes, Dr Atkins. I am real. The only thing is, whilst your science is *real* for everyone, I am only real for the special few. So you have to keep me a secret." Tippy fluttered off Richard Atkins hands and on to Liz's mum's shoulder, making Mrs Atkins hold her breath. Everything was so astonishing.

As they waited to see what Tippy would do next, a humungous snore emerged from Toby. So much for his pledge to stay awake the whole night!

"Hmm, that's reassuring. At least the natural order of things hasn't been thrown entirely off balance! Toby's snoring is as musical and as loud as it ever was. No change there."

"Oh, lighten up Dr Atkins. The only change around here is that you've got me for company."

Serendipity spoke as if her presence was as normal an occurrence as Abigail coming over to spend the weekend.

"Speaking of the natural order of things, I could do with some of what Toby's enjoying right now. There's nothing like a good night's rest."

"Do fairies sleep?" asked Helena.

"Of course we do. How else do you think we manage to stay so cute and perky?" Tippy gave Mrs Atkins a little kiss. "I like you Mrs Atkins."

"Uh, I like you too, I think."

"So when will you go back Tippy? How will you go?"

"I don't know Helena. One magical day like this, I suppose, in some magical way. I've only just got here. Why do we have to talk about me going back! Let's talk about where I'm going to sleep, instead. Hey, Dr Atkins, you need to get some rest too you know. Otherwise *your* natural order will definitely be disturbed. Come on".

"Sleep, yes, of course. We should all go to sleep."

Dr Atkins didn't look like he would sleep in a million years! Wide eyed disbelief was still pasted all over his face. Nevertheless the 'natural order' prevailed and in the wee hours of the morning, The Kowhai household finally fell into an uneasy slumber—Tippy comfortably cuddled up in an old shoebox which Mrs Atkins had filled up with cotton wool,

Toby completely at peace with the world, dreaming of doggie biscuits and marshmallows, Helena and Liz exhausted from the days' excitement and finally,

Dr and Mrs Atkins.

"Chris, are you asleep?" asked Dr Atkins as he adjusted his duvet.

"No, Richard, what is it?"

"Dad always said 'The Kowhai' would bring us a magical future. I wonder if he knew just *how* magical it would be."

# A Different Perspective

BARTHOLOMEW WAS FED up waiting for his breakfast. Liz's mum and Dad were still not awake! Dr Atkins was snoring away to his heart's content. This was totally unacceptable! In all these years Toby had never waited for *any* meal, let alone breakfast, the most important meal of the day! Hmm, he better keep an eye on that thing that was asleep in Elizabeth's room. Last night he'd thought he'd be nice to Liz's new friend. But if it was going to jeopardise his chances of getting his meals on time Toby would have to reconsider!

Finally, his face covered with slobbery licks, Dr Atkins woke up. "Bartholomew, get off me. Toby, stop it. Toby, get down boy".

In the adjoining room, hearing her father's tussle with Tobby, Liz groggily opened her eyes. Was it all a dream, or had she actually met a fairy? Elizabeth still felt quite exhausted.

"Oh, you're awake. Good."

Elizabeth looked to her side. "Good morning, why are you staring at me like that? Don't tell me you thought it was all a dream."

"I thought it was all a dream", said Liz.

"I told you not to say that. Well, think all you want, but I am not a dream. This bed is really comfy you know. I must thank your mum for pumping up the cushions so much."

The Tiny fairy's continuous chatter made Elizabeth smile. "You certainly talk a lot."

"Well, that makes two of us. Come on, let us go and see what is for breakfast."

Just then, Liz's mum and Dad came in. "Is she still there?"

"You bet I am, Mrs Atkins. You'll get used to me soon. I'm not too much trouble, you know. Just flutter around minding my own business. Oh by the way, Mrs Atkins, this shoe box is so comfy. Thanks a lot."

"You're welcome, Tippy. Shall we go down now—it's a lovely day. Lizzy maybe you'd like to take Tippy for a stroll around the Kowhai. "Yes, mum. That'll be nice. I will probably go to Abi's this afternoon. We thought we would do our homework together. Is that Ok?"

"It's perfectly ok, as long as you *do* get some home work done and don't end up listening to MISschief's latest album!!

"Speaking of MISschief'" Dr Atkins looked up from his newspaper, "apparently she's going to be doing a gig in Sheffield sometime in the next year."

"Really? Oh, wow!! Can we go Dad, can we? Is there a picture? Helena almost made her father topple over in her overly zealous attempts to get a glimpse of the newspaper article.

"Can we dad?" chipped in Elizabeth.

"Listen girls. I simply said that MiSschief was *planning* to have a show. Nothing's been confirmed yet. No date, no time or venue and nothing about the tickets. Besides, even if those details were available it wouldn't be for at least another four to five months. So for now, why don't you enjoy that little piece of MISschief?" Dr Atkins looked at Tippy who was perched on the edge of Elizabeth's chair

"Christine, I need to go into town to pick up a few things for the surgery."

"I'll come with you Richard. I need to go to 'Coopers' to print out some labels for tomorrows' open day. Helena you can come with us and exchange your book. Well, Lizzy, you've got the whole house to yourself. Be sure to lock the door before you go out. We'll be back for lunch."

While Elizabeth got dressed, Tippy cast an appreciative glance at her paintings.

"Right, shall we make a move. Where's Toby?" Elizabeth began to make her way downstairs with Tippy nestling on top of her pony tail. "Oh there he is, lazy lumps". Bartholomew was busy being himself, spread out in front of the television, clearly with no intention of wanting to move. Things were perfect. Dr Atkins wasn't home to insist he goes for his morning exercise routine. Best of all, the new flying creature had obviously cast a spell on Elizabeth! She'd forgotten to put the biscuits back into the shelf after breakfast. Well, it wasn't his fault. Biscuits which were carelessly left on the dining table were his!

So there he was, plonked on his favourite rug, tummy a bit too full from ingesting the entire packet of biscuits. Toby was one thoroughly satisfied dog. Now, if only he could enjoy that snooze he'd been planning.

"Tobeeeeee!", yelled Lizzy. "Get up. We're going for a walk. Toby! Oh, I see. Thought you could escape didn't you. Come on you nincompoop. Gosh! Toby you finished a whole packet of biscuits. How could you? You greedy dog! You are most definitely going for an extra run today."

Elizabeth opened the main door and let a disgruntled Bartholomew hobble out. Within minutes though, Toby had his engines in full throttle and was running around the gardens eager to chase a squirrel or two.

"You know, Elizabeth," said Serendipity as they followed Toby, "I was looking at your paintings. You're actually quite good at maths"

"Huh"? Elizabeth looked at Tippy with a puzzled expression. "Usually people who see my pictures say I'm good at painting, Tippy, not Maths!!In fact, nobody has ever told me I'm good at Maths, because I'm not. In fact, just yesterday Ms Fitzgerald told me I'd better get my act together and start 'counting' properly!"

"And you will, Lizzy. I heard what Mrs Fitzgerald said.

"What! You heard? How?"

"I was in your bag silly, remember? Anyway, as I was saying, I think you're good at maths. The city landscape, for instance. The buildings are fine but I can barely see the people. They're just tiny dots. Why don't you make the people look like people, not tiny ants?"

Tippy could sense Elizabeth's indignation rising.

"Tippy, that's preposterous! How can you have people as tall as the skyscrapers they're standing next to? Everything has to be proportionate. They have to be to scale—balanced."

"Exactly, proportion, scale and balance—that's maths. I told you, you understand Mathematics much better than you realise."

"I suppose when you put it that way. But strokes with my paintbrush come naturally to me Tippy. I go blank when I see numbers"

"You know, Elizabeth. Sometimes we can change the way we feel about something by looking at it differently. Instead of telling yourself that you're going to go blank, why don't you tell yourself that you won't? Be more positive? Things aren't always as easy as a stroke of a paintbrush, Liz. And as you realise only too well, no one is good at everything. But if you've got a dream and set your heart on it, anything is possible."

"Do you really think so? I mean, I just don't know how to get my maths grades up"

"For starters tell yourself that you *can do it*. The rest will fall into place. A clear, confident mind can solve many a problem."

Elizabeth smiled at the pun in Tippy's words.

"So what about you, don't fairies have any problems? Is it all a fairy tale for you?"

Just then Toby, who had been busy chasing a rabbit, came up and jumped on to Elizabeth.

"Bartholomew, you are filthy. Get off me! Toby, stop it."

Elizabeth finally managed to fend off Bartholomew. She sent him scampering after a long branch that had fallen off the birch tree that she was resting against.

"He is such a big baby", thought Elizabeth. "He reminds me of Baloo from the Jungle Book. Hey, Baloo and Bartholomew. It even rhymes. They make the perfect pair." Elizabeth chuckled to herself picturing Toby and Baloo dancing to 'Bear Necessities'.

Liz suddenly realised that Toby hadn't given Tippy a chance to answer her question.

"So my fairy friend, is there anything that drives you into frenzy? Where are you, Tippy? Tippy . . ." Elizabeth looked all around expecting to spot Tippy flapping around nearby. Surprisingly there was no sign of the fairy. "Tippy, where are you? Are you playing hide and seek?" Elizabeth jumped when a small bird's nest fell down next to her. She looked up to see something glittering on the branches.

"I'm here" said a familiar voice. Tippy was on the tree. Her wings had managed to accidently dislodge the nest. Thankfully there weren't any eggs in it.

"What are you doing up there? Toby, come back, we have to go home now. You can chase the squirrel later. Well, well, well, so you've finally decided to come down eh?" Tippy was now slightly lower down from where she was previously, but still hesitant to descend any further.

"Tippy . . . , now what's stopping you? Is there something special about this tree? Come on Tippy, let's go home. Tobeeee . . . ! Toby, you're so exasperating sometimes."

Elizabeth sighed and looked at Tippy who was still no closer to the ground. She noticed that the fairy hadn't spoken a word for some time. Looking at her, Elizabeth realized that Tippy had her eyes fixed on Bartholomew. Suddenly the problem dawned on her

"Oh, I get it.! Tippy, you're afraid of Toby, aren't you? That's why you've been keeping your distance every time Toby came near me. Tippy, Toby is just a big baby. He's been chasing a squirrel for the last half an hour. Forget about the squirrel, even a butterfly will be too smart for Toby. Bartholomew is just a really big dog, with an even bigger heart. He wouldn't hurt anyone, Tippy."

Serendipity was not convinced.

"I don't know. I think I'll just let *you* love him for now, Lizzy. I'm afraid he'll mistake me for a butterfly, one day."

"Fine, join me when you're ready. I've got to get home now. Elizabeth started walking towards The Kowhai. Toby followed grumpily, having conceded defeat to the butterfly. Tippy did get home soon after, but no amount of reasoning would convince her to befriend Bartholomew.

Later, Elizabeth made herself a sandwich for lunch and headed off to Abigail's. They spent the afternoon together and managed to tackle English grammar, Geometry and Biology homework. For once Elizabeth didn't grumble about her Mathematics. She thought of Tippy's words—"Be more positive".

"That wasn't too bad, was it Abs", said Elizabeth after the last science question was completed.

"Yeah, except for that diagram in Biology. Sometimes I wish I had your drawing skills. Anyway, let's have a break. Have you listened to MISschief's new song? Abigail switched on the CD player and the music began.

Outside the autumn leaves continued to fall creating a dazzling carpet of fiery reds, pale yellows and terracotta browns. Serendipity fluttered around nearby, watching over Elizabeth, as she would for many years to come.

# *Mirabel*

THE WEEKS WERE passing by swiftly. It was more than a month since 'The Kowhai' welcomed its new 'guest'. Already, Elizabeth's *roommate* was pretty much part of the family and the idea of a fairy at the dinner table no longer seemed that unusual.

With Christmas fast approaching, Primrose High was a hive of activity. Not only was there an extra drive on the part of the teachers to cover the planned curriculum, there was an even more enthusiastic effort from the students to put on the best Christmas show so far.

Every year Primrose High held an entertainment event at Christmas time. It was a showcase for the school's young talent, giving the girls a chance to display their skills in areas like music and the fine arts. More often than not, guests from other schools and colleges also attended the event. A form on the notice board outside Ms Barrymore's office had the names of all the students who would be performing on the night, with spaces for more entries.

Elizabeth was outside in the playground. "So which composition will you be playing, Abi?" asked Elizabeth.

"I'm not playing the violin this year, Liz"

"What! Why not?"

Just then Alison Radcliffe and her *satellites* walked by.

"Well, if it isn't Leonardina . . . So what are you going to be doing Elizabeth, a mural on the stage floor?"

"Oh shut up Alison. I bet you couldn't draw a proper rectangle, if you were asked to," retorted Abigail always ready to speak up for her friend who preferred to let silence speak for itself.

"Oh, I think I could draw a perfect rectangle, thank you. My measurements would be accurate anyway, unlike some others. Heard you're not playing the violin this year, what's up? Got cold feet, did you? Too shy to perform in front of the 'big girls', huh?

"When I think it is necessary to inform you of my decisions, Alison, I will. Till then, I would like you to mind your own business."

Alison walked off in a huff rolling her eyes.

"Gosh! When will she learn, Ms High and Mighty? Just because she has got a great voice, it's no reason to go around taunting others."

"I just ignore her, Abi. Why don't you? Anyway, what's all this about you not playing the violin?"

"Lizzy, I'm going to sing this time," said Abigail almost in a whisper.

"Sing? I never thought you were serious about singing. I'm surprised, Abi".

"Why? I *have* composed a few songs on my own. You know that, Liz. I got thinking and it seems a good idea to do something different. Surprise everyone. What do you think? It's a showcase after all."

Elizabeth was caught off guard. She didn't know what to say. So she blurted out the first thing that came to her.

"Yeah! Go for it Abi, it certainly *will* be a surprise."

"Thanks Liz, I knew you would support me. Listen I've got to go. I promised Ms Cooper I'd discuss the Biology assignment we submitted yesterday. See you later."

Abi ran off. Elizabeth sat down on the nearest bench she could find. Oh no! This was terrible. Abigail Swift singing on stage in front of all those people! In front of Alison Radcliffe! What could she do? What *should* she do? Abi was her best friend.

"Torn apart, eh?"

Elizabeth turned to see Tippy gently glide onto her school bag. Thankfully, there was no one else nearby. So there was no danger of arousing suspicion. Otherwise, the sight of Elizabeth Atkins speaking to her school bag would definitely have raised a few eyebrows!!!

"Oh! Tippy, I am so glad to see you. I don't know what to do . . . Abi just told me she is going to . . .

"Sing" said Tippy before Elizabeth could complete her sentence. "And you don't think this is a good idea because firstly, she can't sing. Secondly, she plays the violin par excellence and you don't see the need for her to display any other talent. Furthermore you don't want the likes of Alison Radcliffe laughing at her. But most of all you don't know what to do about it because you don't want to hurt your best friend".

"How did you know all that?"

"I'm your fairy. I'm meant to know these things."

"Ok, clever cat, what should I do?"

"I don't know"

"What!! You're my fairy friend. It's your job to tell me what to do." Elizabeth looked at Tippy expectantly.

"No, Elizabeth. That is not my job. And that is not what friends do."

Elizabeth was rather taken aback at the sudden vehemence in Tippy's otherwise soft, delicate tone. She also felt slightly uncomfortable that Tippy might have misunderstood her 'plea for help' as more of a command and she listened intently as Tippy continued

"Friends tell each other what they feel in an honest and unselfish way. They believe in their friendship enough to put it to the test. Friends stay friends forever. So Elizabeth, it certainly is NOT my job to tell you what to do. It is, however, my *choice* to be your friend. Now what you decide to do about Abi, is your choice, not mine. Think about it. I'll see you at home."

Serendipity flew off leaving some golden dust in the air as she lifted away.

"I suppose it did sound like a Bossy Boots," thought Elizabeth. "I must apologise to Tippy. She shouldn't think that I take her for granted. Besides, she's right. What's the point if Tippy tells me what to do? I have to decide myself."

Serendipity's words came back to Elizabeth. Friends were 'open, honest and unselfish'. Was she being selfish by discouraging Abigail? No, definitely not. Elizabeth had nothing to gain, but Abi had so much to lose. Wasn't it Liz's duty to protect Abi or at least try? Elizabeth pondered over these questions for a few more minutes. The answer was clear to her. Tippy hadn't told Elizabeth what to do. But she had definitely set her thoughts moving in the right direction.

It was almost home time. Before she left, Elizabeth had to collect her Biology assignment from Ms Cooper.

"Liz", somebody tugged on Liz's shirt. "It's is only me Elizabeth. I was wondering whether you could do me a really big favour."

It was Mirabel Mitchell, smiling as usual.

"Of course, Mirabel, I'll do anything you want. What is it?" asked Liz.

"Could you collect my science assignment from Ms Cooper for me please? You see, I have to rush home early. My Mum's not doing too well. I've got to pick up her medicine and the pharmacy only works till half three on Fridays."

"That's not a problem at all, Mirabel. I hope your mum's not too ill."

"No, no . . . It's just a bad flu, nothing serious. I just don't want her going out on her own to get the tablets. Thanks a bunch, Liz. I already asked Ms Cooper if someone could collect my assignment for me, and she's fine with it." Mirabel squeezed Liz's hands. "I hope I've done alright. I guess I'll have to wait till Monday to find out. Thanks again Elizabeth, have a good weekend."

"You're most welcome, Mirabel." Elizabeth waved to Mirabel as she ran off. In spite of the many occasions that Mirabel had joined Abi and Elizabeth for lunch, Liz realized that the conversation they'd just had was probably the longest. Mirabel was pretty much as quiet as she was on the first day of school.

As she proceeded to Ms Cooper's office, Elizabeth had an idea. Her mum did mention that Toby needed some cough mixture. Maybe she could go into town on her way home and pick up Toby's medicine. More importantly, maybe she could stop at Mirabel's place and give her the assignment. It would be a surprise for Mirabel and everyone knew how keen Mirabel was as far as any science work was concerned. The problem was, Elizabeth didn't know Mirabel's address even though she knew it was near town. Maybe Ms Cooper could help. Elizabeth knocked on Ms Cooper's door.

"Come in" came the familiar voice. Ms Cooper was at her table marking the students' work. "Hmm Elizabeth, some decent work there, I must say. The diagrams are perfect as usual. I do think you could go into a bit more detail as far as the characteristics of amphibians go though. Anyway, here's your work."

"Thank you, Ms. Uh . . . Ms Cooper, Mirabel asked me . . ."

"Oh yes, I almost forgot. Mirabel did mention that you would come to collect her assignment. Here you go."

Elizabeth put both the assignments into her bag.

"Ms. Cooper, there's just one more thing. I was wondering whether you could help me get Mirabel's address. You see, I thought I could give her the assignment this evening, so that she wouldn't have to wait until Monday. I don't think Ms Wilkinson would give me her address unless she knew it is with your permission."

"That's a kind thought, Liz. I'm sure Mirabel would be pleased. I bet she's very eager to find out how she's done especially since the assignment is based on animals. She wants to be a vet, you know."

"Really . . . ?"

"Yes. So she keeps telling me. Anyway come along, let's go and see if we can convince Ms Wilkinson to divulge some very confidential information from the school data base!"

Elizabeth chuckled, as Ms Cooper tiptoed across the room pretending to be on a top secret mission. Soon Mirabel's address was no longer *classified* information.

Walking out of the office, Elizabeth opened the side pouch of her school bag. She took out her cell phone. Elizabeth had strict orders from her mum and dad that the phone was only meant to be used for 'important' calls, not to yap endlessly with Abi about the umpteen number of insignificant things they'd forgotten to discuss during school hours!

Elizabeth called her mum and told her that she would be late coming home.

"If you could go to 'Whiskers and Paws', that'd be great. Liz. I was planning to go myself, but if you're going into town, you might as well pick it up."

"Bye, mum, see you at tea time. Oh! By the way, here's Mirabel's address and phone number in case you have to call me." Liz hung up and thanked Ms Wilkinson. As she walked down the corridor, she suddenly remembered Abi. Well, Abi would have to wait. She had to do this for Mirabel now. Anyway it was Friday. Maybe she could meet up with Abi over the weekend.

Outside, the sky was already dark—a typical late November afternoon. For a moment, Elizabeth wondered if she had been too hasty. The cold winter air and the dismal atmosphere made her wish she was at home with Toby. But the moment passed. Liz knew that sweet Mirabel would be delighted to see her 'A' grade assignment. She caught the short route bus and got out at Hedgewood Street as per the address she'd got from school. This was the first time that Liz had travelled to this part of the town. The Kowhai was at the opposite end.

She glanced at her watch. Twenty minutes. Not bad. It took Liz and Abi almost that long to get to school by school bus. Liz had expected the journey to take longer. She looked all around. It was quiet, although a few shops next to the bus stop were open. Elizabeth checked the address again—Greetby Buildings, 11A Block 2. It sounded like a block of flats. An elderly couple were waiting at the bus top. Elizabeth asked them if they knew the address.

"You're not far at all, love" said the lady. "Just walk down the road opposite the florist and turn left. The building's right there."

Elizabeth thanked them and followed the lady's instructions. Sure enough, before long she was standing in front of two apartment buildings. There was a large gate which opened into what appeared to be a common garden for the occupants. On the whole, the structure wasn't that big. Each block of flats had only two floors.

The building next to the entrance was Block 1. So Elizabeth walked to Block 2. The main door to the lobby was locked. Liz noticed a set of switches with numbers from 11A to 20 A. She realised that to enter she had to be granted permission through the intercom. Elizabeth pressed the button next to 11A. A muffled voice came through the speaker. "Yes, who is it?"

"My name's Elizabeth Atkins. Is this Mirabel Mitchell's home?"

"Lizzy, I can't believe it. Wait there, I'm coming down."

Elizabeth heard a click and knew that the door was open. As soon as she went in, she heard hurried footsteps rushing down a flight of steps. Elizabeth looked up and saw Mirabel, eyes as wide as saucers, bare-footed wearing an old T shirt and pyjamas.

"I can't believe this, what are you doing here, Elizabeth? Is everything ok? Are you on your own? Gosh! I can't believe this. Are you Ok?"

"Mirabel, sh . . . !!!!" Elizabeth put her hand over Mirabel's mouth in an attempt to calm her down.

"Everything's fine, Mirabel, now relax. I wanted to surprise you, not shock you."

"Ooh silly me . . . I'm not shocked. I mean, I *am* shocked, but now that I know you're ok, I am happily shocked," said Mirabel giving Elizabeth a hug. Now come on up. My mum's waiting."

Elizabeth followed Mirabel up the stairs. A little girl, probably seven or eight years old was standing outside one of the flats.

"Mummy, they're here. Oooh . . . she's really stylish Mummy, look."

Elizabeth looked at Mirabel slightly bemused, not knowing what to make of the youngster's animated prattle.

"That's my little sister, Rebecca. Beware, Elizabeth. She's bound to stick to you like superglue the moment you walk in. Becky is in awe of the 'big girls' that I go to school with, especially the ones I call my friends."

They were now in front of Mirabel's flat. A lady with short brown hair, wearing a floral print blouse and white skirt came up to Elizabeth.

"Come in darling. It's so lovely to meet you. Mirabel has told us so much about her best friend, Elizabeth.

With these loving words was an equally welcoming smile. This lady was unmistakably Mirabel's mother. Elizabeth would have loved to tell Mirabel's mum that she knew so much about them too, but Mirabel had disclosed very little about her family. In fact, Mirabel had disclosed very little about *anything at all* since she joined school. She was content just getting on with her work, no trouble to anyone. And, to think that she considered Elizabeth her 'best friend'. Liz really didn't know what to say.

"Thank you Mrs Mitchell. I'm thrilled to be here too. Hello Rebecca. That's a nice dress you're wearing". Elizabeth held out her hand. Of course, her new admirer jumped at the opportunity.

"I know. It's my favourite. Mum made it for me. Let's go in now, mum. I want to show Elizabeth my pictures." Rebecca gripped Liz's hand and led her into the living room. The room was *much* smaller than the reception room at the Kowhai. It had the basic requirements—a sofa, an armchair and a small television set.

"Do sit down, Elizabeth", said Mirabel pointing to the sofa. "So why are you here? Please . . . I'm dying of curiosity. How did you get my address?"

"Well, I got your address with Ms Cooper's help. I hope you don't mind. I wanted to give you this." Elizabeth took the marked assignment out of her book bag and handed it to Mirabel. "It's your science report"

Mirabel's face lit up. "Oh wow, that's so kind of you Lizzy. You needn't have gone to all this trouble. I would have waited till Monday."

"Mirabel, it's no trouble at all. I wanted to do it. Now I just hope you've done as well as you always do."

Mirabel opened the folder and saw that Ms Cooper had given her an 'A'

"Mummy, I've got an 'A'." Mirabel jumped up and hugged Elizabeth." Liz, you don't know how much this means to me. Thank you, thank you, and thank you".

"I think I do know how much it means to you Mirabel. It's written all over your face," said Elizabeth returning Mirabel's hug.

"It's very kind of you dear, coming all the way. Especially, in such miserable weather. Now, why don't I get you something to drink? Some hot cocoa perhaps. Becky will want some too. She's been pestering me for a long time now. Becky ... Becky come here, love. Where's she gone to now? She was here a minute ago."

The little chatterbox suddenly reappeared from behind one of the curtains. She pushed Mirabel aside and sat down next to Elizabeth. Rebecca was holding on to a picture of some sort. Elizabeth couldn't see it clearly.

"You know Elizabeth; you don't have to call me Rebecca. You can call me Becky if you like because you're Bel's friend. Only friends can call me Becky. I don't like Robbie's friends calling me Becky. They're boys. I don't like boys. Do you like boys Elizabeth?"

"Becky, keep quiet! You talk too much. Don't irritate Elizabeth with your endless questions".

Elizabeth smiled. "It's ok Mrs Mitchell. I've got a younger sister too. And believe me; she *hardly ever* wants to ask me any questions! Says I'm not intelligent enough! So this is quite refreshing for a change."

Elizabeth put her arm over Rebecca's shoulder. "I would love to call you Becky. Thank you. I certainly feel very special. As for whether I like boys … hmm … I haven't really thought about it. My dad's a boy. I like *him*. So I guess all boys aren't bad."

"OK. That's enough now Becky", said Mrs Mitchell. "Now come here and help me get the hot chocolate."

"I'll get the drinks, mum. Hello Elizabeth. I'm Robbie."

A boy a few years older than Elizabeth and Mirabel came out of one of the adjoining rooms.

"Lizzy, this is my brother, Robert. He's in college now."

Robert shook Elizabeth's hand.

"So, hot chocolate for everyone then." Robbie walked into the tiny kitchen. Rebecca had spread her picture out for Elizabeth. It was a vase with lots of multicoloured flowers.

RASHMI KAIMAL

"Very nice, Becky," Elizabeth nodded approvingly. "Do you like colouring?"

"Oh I love it. Bel, shall we show Elizabeth all my other pictures. Come on Elizabeth." Rebecca pulled Elizabeth towards one of the bedrooms.

"I warned you", Mirabel whispered to Elizabeth, "At this rate you won't be able to go home".

"It's ok. Look at how excited she is."

The bedroom had a double bed and a table with Mirabel's books on it.

"This is actually my room Elizabeth. I share it with Mirabel and mum because I love them. All those pictures are mine. What do you think?"

Unlike Elizabeth, the seven year old 'artist' let her imagination flow with no consideration whatsoever for 'scale and proportion!! An ocean with fish as big as the ships sailing past them, people taller than the trees in their garden! Furthermore, Rebecca was still getting the hang of colouring within the lines. But then, those flaws *were* the pictures' greatest merits. The innocence, effort and pride with which Becky regarded her masterpieces made them exactly that—Masterpieces.

"I think you could become a famous artist one day, Becky."

"Mirabel says you're going to become a famous artist. Are you?"

"That's very kind of you Mirabel. I do enjoy art. But I think I'm going to have to get through high school before I can think of becoming famous."

Robbie's voice rang out through the living room.

"How about some cookies with your hot chocolate, folks?"

Soon they were all gulping down delicious hot chocolate with homemade cookies. "These cookies are delicious Mrs Mitchell" said Liz as a cookie melted in her mouth. Elizabeth was touched when she heard Mrs Mitchell's account of how excited Mirabel was the day Liz shared her 'Delicio' ice cream with her.

"Mirabel has always wanted to taste 'Delicio'. Now, Rebecca is pestering me to get some for her as well."

"No, I'm not Mummy. Dad is going to buy some when he comes home next time" chipped in Becky.

"Comes home next time?"

Elizabeth looked at Mirabel. "Elizabeth, my dad works in Dover. He works for a transportation company and his job involves a lot of travel across the channel into France and Europe, we only to get to see him every couple of months."

"You must miss him . . ."

"Of course we do," said Mirabel. "But hey, sometimes that's just the way it is. Besides, it makes things extra special when Dad does come home."

Elizabeth looked at Robert who was putting more cookies on to the plate. With the plate of biscuits almost empty,

RASHMI KAIMAL

Elizabeth listened to Becky's description of how hilarious the book that she just read was, followed by Becky's rendition of a song that her class would be singing for Assembly the next day, and finally, browsed through Becky's baby photo album which she showed off proudly perched on Elizabeth's lap.

"I warned you Lizzy, she won't let you off easily. Come on Becky, that's enough about you. Elizabeth must be fed up."

"Oh! Don't worry Mirabel. I thoroughly enjoyed that, Becky. In fact I enjoyed everything here. I have never felt so much at home."

"It's a pleasure to have you here", said Mirabel's mum.

"Mirabel, I think I better make a move now. Goodness! It's almost 6 'o' clock. I better call my dad."

"Here, you can use this phone, Liz."

Mirabel passed Elizabeth a handset before she could take her own phone out. Liz dialled her home number.

"Hello, Mum. Is Daddy home?"

"Actually he's not, why?"

"I was just wondering whether he could pick me up. Will he be long?"

"I don't think so. In fact he should be waiting in front of Mirabel's house round about now."

"Huh!! How . . ."

"I'll tell you later. Don't spend too much time on the phone." Elizabeth's sudden confusion brought looks of concern on the others' faces.

"Is everything ok, Liz?" Mirabel asked once Liz had put the receiver down.

"Oh it is better than ok. My dad is actually waiting downstairs. I'm just surprised. How did he know . . . oh, yes, I remember, I gave mum your address and telephone number when I called to let her know that I'd be coming here."

"Isn't that a lovely surprise? In any case, Elizabeth, we wouldn't have let you go home on your own. Robbie would have taken you without a doubt, wouldn't you Robbie?"

"Of course I would have, mum. Come on let's all go down and meet Liz's dad."

Mirabel's mum hugged Elizabeth. "I won't come down right now Elizabeth, but do give my regards to your father and come again soon. It's been lovely having you."

Mrs Mitchell was full of genuine warmth and affection. In spite of their modest dwellings and the few modern conveniences they enjoyed, the Mitchells had something so priceless that it made the likes of Alison Radcliffe look like paupers! They cared for one another in a way that made total strangers feel like family.

Dr Atkins was waiting in his car just outside the gate. On seeing Elizabeth and her friends, he got out and walked up to them extending his hand out to Robbie.

"Good evening, Sir."

"Good evening to you too, uh . . ."

"It's Robbie, sir—Robert actually."

"Well, good evening Robert and please don't call me 'sir'. Just call me Richard. And you must be Mirabel."

Liz's father patted Mirabel on her shoulder and then noticed a small pony tail trying to hide behind her.

"Oh, this must be the little princess that we read about in the news. Isn't that so, Lizzy?"

"Yes, Dad, this is Princess Rebecca," said Elizabeth pulling Becky out from behind Mirabel. "But I am sure she will let you call her Becky, won't you Becky? Please . . . he's a good boy, promise." Rebecca smiled.

"Well, that's the longest she's kept quiet in the past few hours, anyway," teased Robbie.

After thanking them all once again, Elizabeth hugged Mirabel and Becky and got into the car. A few minutes into the drive, Elizabeth put her head on to her dad's shoulder.

"Daddy,"

"Yes, Liz?"

"Daddy, you won't go away, will you?"

"Huh? Why would I go away? Lizzy, what has gotten into you?"

"I love you Dad."

"I know, sweetheart. I love you too. But why the sudden rush of emotion?"

"I'm just happy, Dad."

"Oh, ok. That makes a lot of sense. You've got tears in your eyes *because you're happy*? Gosh! I always tell your mum I don't understand women. And I have to live with three of them."

"Actually, make that four Dr Atkins," came a soft voice from somewhere in the back seat.

"Tippy, when did you get here?"

"I've been here a while."

"So why is Lizzy so upset?

"Elizabeth told you Dr Atkins, she's not upset, just happy."

Dr Atkins sighed and shook his head.

"Well, as long as its '*love and happiness*' that's causing the watery eyes and not a high temperature, I'm happy too. You've had a long day Liz, try and get some rest."

Tippy flew onto Elizabeth's lap.

"Your Dad's right, Lizzy. Lizzy . . . ?"

There was no reply. Elizabeth had fallen asleep with her head resting on Dr Atkins's shoulder.

# *Broken Strings* 7

"DID YOU ENJOY yourself at Mirabel's place, Liz?"

Serendipity was sitting on one of the cotton wool balls in her shoe box bed, her tiny feet dangling playfully over one side of the box. Elizabeth was just getting out of bed, stretching as she flung off the duvet. She was quiet, deep in thought.

"Of course I did, Tippy. It's not how much I enjoyed myself, though. I mean, I know Helena and I are very lucky and Dad and Mum always tell us we shouldn't take anything for granted. But yesterday, when I heard that onc scoop of 'Delicio' meant so much to Mirabel and that Becky still hadn't even tasted it, I realised just how much I *do* take for granted. No wonder Mirabel is so quiet in school. She probably feels too embarrassed to join in, especially when the conversations are about MISschief, fashion and movies."

"Yes, maybe," said Tippy. "On the other hand, maybe Mirabel doesn't feel the conversation is worth her while to contribute to. She's a sensible girl, Lizzy, with her heart set on making the most of her scholarship. You know she wants to become a vet. Maybe she doesn't want any distractions and would rather stay focused than fill her head with dreams she can't afford. That certainly doesn't mean that she's unhappy."

"I suppose so. Anyway I am happy to have a friend like her. Oh, speaking of friends, Tippy, I am sorry for sounding rather bossy yesterday. I didn't mean to. You know, about Abi."

"Oh, forget about it. I know you didn't mean to be rude. You were just caught off guard when Abi told you she wanted to sing. I understand. What about you, Liz. Have you thought about it? What are you going to do?"

"I'm going to speak to her after breakfast. I want what's best for her, Tippy. That's why I don't want her to sing. I'm sure Abi will understand. I hope she will."

They made their way downstairs. "I think you're doing the right thing, Lizzy . . . good luck!"

After a quick breakfast, Elizabeth set off for Abigail's house. She locked the door behind her. Helena and her mum had taken Toby for a walk and her dad had gone to town to get Toby the medicine which Elizabeth had forgotten.

"We can really depend on you, Liz" her Dad had teased before he left.

Elizabeth smiled to herself as she thought of her reply.

"I was so intent on catching the right bus, Dad. That's why I forgot. Imagine how worried you would have been if I had caught the wrong bus to Mirabel's place. Imagine that!! You and mum worried sick. Surely, you can understand . . ."

Elizabeth's parents looked at her and frowned.

"Darling, that's why we've bought you a phone!!!"

"Ok fine. You win. Anyway, Toby knows he can depend on me, don't you Tobykins, whether I forget his medicines or not." Toby came lumbering up to Elizabeth and slobbered her face with a truck load of doggy licks.

Elizabeth wondered if Abi would know that she could depend on her. Would she trust Elizabeth's judgement? She would just have to wait and see. When Elizabeth arrived at Abi's house, Abi's mother opened the door.

"Lizzy, what a surprise! Come on in. Abigail is up and about somewhere" said Abigail's mum as Liz walked into the foyer.

"Abi, you've got a visitor".

"Coming mum, who is it?" Abi looked down from the landing.

"Lizzy you're up early, I'm still in my pyjamas. Come on up. Where is Toby? He usually tags along whenever you come over."

"He's gone for a walk with Mum and Helena. His cough isn't doing too good. Dad is getting him more medicine, hopefully that will help. I can't believe that Toby is going to be eight."

Abi was standing next to her hi-fi looking at some music sheets.

"Yeah, how time flies." Abi looked up from at Elizabeth.

"Liz, I was just going through some songs for next week. Can you help me select something which suits my voice?"

"Yes umm . . . about that, Abi. That's really the reason why I wanted to talk to you this early in the morning."

"Oh! What is it?"

"Well, uh . . . uh . . . I had a good think about what you asked me, you know, whether it was a good idea for you to sing instead of play the violin.

The more I think about it, Abi, I feel you should stick to the violin. I mean you are simply superb."

"Thanks for the compliment, Liz. But as I said, everyone knows that I can play the violin. I want to do something different this time."

Elizabeth was struggling to find the right words. How could she tell Abi her true feelings without hurting her? It wasn't that Abi couldn't sing at all. She could definitely hum a few tunes without going off key, but Elizabeth knew that was not good enough for the talent show. Not with girls like Alison Radcliffe who had started voice coaching sessions since the age of three. Abigail noticed Elizabeth's uneasiness.

"Liz, what is it? I know what you're thinking, Liz. And believe me; I'm aware that my singing is not as good as some of the others. But this is not a competition, so why not give it a go? I don't have anything to lose . . ."

"But Abi, this is the first time you will be able to display your skills to such a large audience and Ms Barrymore said there may be guests from other schools and colleges. So why do you want to do something different now?"

Elizabeth's voice and expression spoke of her frustration. Why couldn't Abi see it? She *did* have so much to lose. Everyone would remember her as a girl who 'thought' she could sing. Abi would be the subject of ridicule.

"Lizzy," said Abi in a low voice. "You don't want me to sing, do you? I see it now. It's not that you want me to play the violin; you just don't want me to sing. That's what it is."

"No, Abi, listen, it's not like that."

Abi wasn't listening.

"Am I that bad, so bad that you would find it embarrassing?" There were tears in Abi's eyes.

"Listen, Abi, I just want what is best for you." Elizabeth tried to put her arm on Abigail's shoulder. But Abi's expression was distant and sullen.

"Yes, I know. I thought you would support me though. Isn't that what friends do?

"But I do support you Abi, I do. It is just . . ." Abi stopped her mid sentence.

"I don't want your advice, Liz . . . I'll just have to do what I have to do whether you agree or not."

"Abi, I'm sorry."

Abigail shrugged her shoulders dismissively.

"I better go now."

Abigail didn't stop her and Liz made her way downstairs. Abi followed quietly. They were at the front door now.

"Bye, Liz".

The door closed and Elizabeth walked up to the gate. Tears were streaming down her face. Her mind was in a whirl. Everything had gone so terribly wrong.

"Hi there, cry baby" it was Tippy chirpy as usual.

"Tippy, how can you say that when you know how awful I feel? Abi is my best friend."

"Well, if she's your best friend you shouldn't be crying."

"Why not, Abi was upset. She was angry with me."

Tippy fluttered onto Elizabeth's hand.

"So what, don't you feel upset and angry at times? That will soon pass. Just let things be. If you are best friends, you will remain best friends."

"Do you really think so, Tippy?"

"I *know* so, Liz. Now wipe your eyes, let's go find Toby."

"I see you're beginning to like Toby."

"No, I don't. All I said is that we should go and look for him."

Elizabeth grinned wiping her face.

"You do like Toby now"

"No, I don't."

"Yes, you do."

"No, I don't, I'm terrified of him."

"Oh yes, you do." Elizabeth persisted.

"Oh, stop it"

Off they went up the slope to the Kowhai, Elizabeth shivering as the cold wind brushed against her.

# Row, Row, Row
# Your Boat ...

LATER THAT DAY Christine Atkins found Elizabeth sitting at her desk staring out through her window with a vacant expression. A note book was lying open in front of her.

"I am assuming that open book in front of you is homework for Monday, Liz. You certainly won't get it done if you continue to study what's going on outside your bedroom window—unless of course *that* is the topic."

"Huh? Oh! Hello mum. Yes, well . . ."

"Lizzy, what's the matter darling? Elizabeth's eyes were red and a half empty box of tissues fell off her lap as she turned to look at her mother. "Why are you so upset, Elizabeth?"

Mrs Atkins went up to her daughter and put an arm around her. "Come on now, there's nothing that you can't tell your mother."

"Or your father", Dr Atkins had just come upstairs into Liz's room.

"That's right, you know, Lizzy. Your mum and dad will always be your best friends.

"You can depend on us. What is making you so upset? It is not like you to sit and brood." Elizabeth dried her eyes.

"I know I can, Dad. It's just that I don't think you can help. I don't think anyone can. It's about Abigail."

Elizabeth told her parents about the events of the previous day, how Abi felt let down by Liz's advice. "I don't think she's going to forgive me."

"Why should she forgive you, Liz?" said Dr Atkins. "You didn't say what you said to hurt her, did you? So what is there to forgive?"

"Exactly, Liz", said her mum. "You just do things and say things in good faith, and then you shouldn't worry about the result. Sweetheart, we don't have any control over how others feel, as long as we've only done things to help them, nothing else matters. It shouldn't."

"These are little lessons in life, Liz. They make you a stronger person." Richard Atkins gave his daughter a hug. "Now let's go downstairs. Helena has been pestering me to go to 'Willow Park'. The lake will be beautiful in this weather. It's cold, but it's still bright and I am sure a boat ride will cheer you up. Now off my shoulder, Tippy, we're going sailing!"

Everyone clambered into Dr Atkins's station wagon, which had a special compartment for Bartholomew to spread himself out. 'Willow Park' was about a forty minute drive from Matlock village. When they arrived at the park, they saw there were hardly any people. In spite of the weather being relatively mild, for December, the kids play area was not pulsating with the usual humdrum and excitement.

"Shall we have lunch first or eat after the boat ride?" asked Liz's Dad.

"Let's go on the boat, first, Dad, please," Helena was jumping around as usual with Toby joining in.

"Yes, that should be Ok, Richard. We all had a late breakfast. So lunch can wait."

They went to the lakeside pier to wait for the next boat. Two large tourist boats were already anchored with some people getting off. One of the guards on board the boat told Dr Atkins that it was due to go out in the next ten minutes and asked them to board if they were interested in a ride.

Seeing as it was a clear sky with no forecast for rain, they decided to sit on the open upper deck. "Oohh!!!", shivered Christine Atkins, "Is this a good idea? Sunny or not, it is soooo cold."

"Don't be such a spoilt sport, Chris. Just rub your hands together and you'll be fine." Dr Atkins threw his scarf over to his wife.

"How romantic, aren't your mum and dad just the perfect couple?" said Tippy.

The boat moved on and everyone gasped as the cold wind rushed on to their faces. None of the other passengers wanted to brave the chill, so they were seated in the covered cabin down below. This worked out well because Tippy's antics went unnoticed.

"How beautiful the lake is even in the winter!" remarked Elizabeth.

"Ah! The artist speaks." Dr Atkins looked at his daughter lovingly.

"Speaking of the artist" said Liz's mum, "how are you getting on with Maths? Has *the artist* managed to find anything colourful about numbers yet?"

"Well, I wouldn't go that far, mum. Maths is anything but colourful to me. I've realized that there is no escape though, so I am determined to go about it as best as I can. Most of all to stop moaning, thanks to Tippy."

"Good for you. Remember what we always tell you. Just try your best."

"Mum, can you hold this bobble, please. I've got a headache. Dad, look at those swans."

"What's wrong with the bobble, Helena, Is it too tight?"

"Yes. Anyway, I don't want it anymore."

"Your hair is going to be all over the place, Helena. What's the point? We're going to have it cut short if you're not able to take care of it." Christine Atkins opened her handbag to put the bobble in, when Tippy flew up to her.

"Toby, those swans do not speak your language." Bartholomew was barking his head off as the swans swam past. Elizabeth went up to him and stroked his head.

"I wish I could understand what he's telling them. Be quiet, Toby. The other passengers are not going to like the racket you're making."

"I'm so pretty, oh so pretty, la . . . la . . . la . . . la . . ." Everyone turned to see Tippy balancing on the edge of the railing with Helena's bobble tied around her tiny waist.

"Isn't it better as a belt? Don't I have a marvellous fashion sense?"

"Tippy, it is simply stunning. Now be careful. Could you please come off those railings?"

"Oh! Don't worry Dr Atkins. I can fly you know." Tippy suddenly swayed to one side. "Oops!!Actually this belt is rather heavy."

"Tippy, please take it off and come off the railings. You're making me nervous."

"Fine, I'll take it off since its causing so much stress!! Thank you Mrs Atkins. Here, you can put it into your handbag."

Just then a sudden gust of wind shook the boat and Tippy lost her balance. The weight of the bobble around her waist meant that her attempts to fly as she fell overboard were futile. The tiny fairy fell into the water.

"Tippeee!!!" Elizabeth screamed.

"Oh no, Richard, what do we do?

"Daddy do something", Helena was already in tears. There was a huge splash which startled them all.

"Toby, it's Toby, he's jumped in."

Two of the passengers from the lower deck, both young men, had rushed up hearing Elizabeth's screams. "Our dog has fallen overboard, we need help."

The two men walked towards Dr Atkins.

"Toby, Toby . . ." Elizabeth and Helena were still screaming for Toby, who had dived under water.

"The water is freezing, he won't survive . . ." Christine Atkins's face was pale with anxiety. Just then Toby's head bobbed out of the water. He was alive but was struggling to stay on the surface.

"I'm going in, Christine," said Dr Atkins.

"That's alright sir. We've got things covered." The two men were already in their life jackets, prepared to dive in. Before Liz's father could react, they had jumped into the water and within seconds, reached Toby. Between the two of them, they were able to support his weight in the water and harness him to the life raft.

At the request of the captain of the boat, the other passengers had remained in their cabin in order to adhere to safety regulations. Last thing they needed was another accident. They watched intently as Toby was hauled up followed by her rescuers.

The poor dog collapsed on the floor exhausted, dazed and shivering. The boat was already moving full speed to the Jetty. The captain had instructed the on shore team that paramedics were required on arrival. The next ten minutes seemed like an eternity. Blankets, shawls, sweaters, scarves—every piece of warm cloth available was given to Toby by the passengers who wanted to help in any way possible to keep him alive.

Meanwhile, Dr Atkins was with the two men checking their pulse and making sure that there were no signs of hypothermia.

"I must say you are in pretty good shape. Those waters must be freezing. How did you do this so effortlessly . . . ? I mean you're not even shivering."

"University swimming, Sir, I'm Tom and this is my pal David."

"Well, it is certainly a privilege to meet you both. We can't thank you enough for plunging in without even a second thought for your own safety. And please don't call me 'sir', I'm Richard. Look we've reached the pier. Excuse me."

Dr Atkins went up to Toby.

"Dad, he's still shivering and his breathing is very heavy", said Elizabeth. Dr Atkins knew they needed to contact Toby's vet, Dr Mathew Baldwin immediately.

"Christine, did you get through to Mathew?"

"I tried, Richard, but the signal is rather weak."

Elizabeth continued to stroke Toby. She gasped when something moved from under his collar.

"Tippy," Elizabeth's voice was a whisper, full of astonishment. "Toby saved you . . . Dad, Mum, Helena, look . . ."

"Oh for God's sake Liz, quieten down. I don't want anyone else to notice me."

"You can talk, you're ok"

"I was ok from the minute Toby brought me back to surface. Fairies are pretty nifty swimmers, you know. It was just the weight of the awful bobble that got in the way." By then, Elizabeth's mum, dad and Helena had rushed up concerned that Toby's condition had worsened.

"What is it, Liz, is Toby ok?"

"It's not Toby, mum. Look down."

"Hello, I'm back." Still clinging to Toby, Serendipity winked at them.

"Tippy . . . , what a relief, we thought we'd lost you. Now if only I could speak to Mathew."

Mrs Atkins tried the number again and managed to get through. "Right, he is on his way to the surgery," said Dr Atkins after speaking to Toby's Doctor.

"Liz, Helena, stay with mum. I'll go with Toby, Chris, you follow me in the car." Elizabeth nodded. Her eyes were already brimming up. This was a nightmare. She watched as the paramedics lifted Toby into the ambulance. Dr Atkins gave both his daughters a kiss and climbed in beside Toby. Seeing the vehicle move off, Elizabeth stood transfixed. Tippy flew up to her and rested her soft wings against Lizzy's tear stained face. The silence spoke volumes—the affection and anxiety they felt for Bartholomew. Elizabeth knew it was going to be a very long night.

# *The Four Seasons*

AT THE ANIMAL Hospital, Toby was immediately taken to a specialist unit. After half an hour, Dr Baldwin . . . came up to Liz's father.

"His temperature is almost back to normal, but we have to take extra precautions to maintain it. What's worrying me though is his airway. You know the cough was already troubling Toby. His lungs are still very congested. Each breath is taking a lot out of him. We're doing everything we can, Richard, but it's too early to say. Bartholomew is a fighter, Liz," he continued going up to Elizabeth.

"The thing is, his age is catching up too and that's another challenge. Let's stay positive, though. As I said, he is a fighter. Why don't you go home now and get some rest? There is nothing much you can do here. Toby is in good hands and we'll keep you informed."

"Thank you Mathew, "said Dr Atkins. "Phew, what a day. Are you sure there's nothing we can do?"

"I'm sure Richard. I'll see you in the morning and will definitely let you know if there's any change in Toby's condition."

The night was longer than Elizabeth had imagined. Still, morning eventually came and Dr Atkins went to the surgery first thing to check on Toby. There wasn't much change in Toby's condition.

"We've got to stay positive, Lizzy. Toby isn't any worse. That's a good point."

"I'm scared for him, Dad. I can't imagine what we'd do if something happened to him."

"Don't cry, Lizzy," Helena ran up to her sister and hugged her as tight as she could. "Toby's going to be fine, isn't he mum?"

Helena looked at her mother hoping for the reassurance that they both needed.

"Come here, sweethearts." Helena and Elizabeth sat down next to their mum. Mrs Atkins put her arms around both of them.

"I wish I could tell you for certain that he will be OK. But I can't. Toby is getting old and we don't know if his body will cope. All we can do is pray for him and hope for the best. Now why don't you go for a walk and get some fresh air. It'll be a distraction. Dad has already informed school that you won't be going today." Mrs Atkins stood up. "I need some bread and milk so the three of you can go into the village and buy some."

"That's a good idea, Mrs Atkins. No point sitting here and brooding." The previous day's adventure hadn't doused Tippy's spirits. She was chirpier than ever.

"Alright, I suppose it's better than sitting at home. Dad, does that mean that you've told the school about the accident?" Elizabeth enquired.

"Well," Dr Atkins looked up, putting his cup of coffee on the dining table. "I did inform the school of the mishap, but only briefly. I'm having a tough time trying to conjure up reasons why our well trained, intelligent dog would jump into a lake of icy water! I mean everyone wants to know how it happened. Imagine telling them that Bartholomew jumped in to rescue a fairy!"

Tippy fluttered onto Dr Atkins shoulder.

"Hee, hee . . . Yeah they'll think you're off your rocker. Can you imagine the headlines in the newspaper?

"Well known Doctor Goes Bonkers!!'

She chuckled as she flew up to Elizabeth.

"Come on girls. We've got to buy some milk."

Helena decided to stay at home and help her mum in the kitchen. As they trudged down the hill to the village, Tippy tried to divert Elizabeth's thoughts from dwelling on Toby.

"Liz, look at that Robin Redbreast. The way it's perched on that tree with the snow in the background, doesn't it remind you of a Christmas card?"

Elizabeth nodded but she was not in the frame of mind to appreciate the scenery. They were soon at 'Barlows', the village newsagents. The door chime rang as Elizabeth entered the shop with Tippy safely hidden in her pocket.

"Hello Elizabeth. I haven't seen you for some time now. How are you keeping, love. Come here. Let's have a good look at you."

Mrs Barlow was a lovely lady in her early sixties, who had known Liz since she was a toddler. The shop was famous in the village for its cream cakes and Mrs Barlow always said her robust frame and plump rosy cheeks were a result of having to make sure that every single batch was perfect for her customers!! In fact, when Liz approached the counter, she saw that a new batch was just being placed on the rack.

"I just tasted one of the cakes to make sure they're exactly how I like them. Here, why don't you try one, Liz."

Mrs Barlow licked the last bit of cream off her fingertips and offered a piece of cake to Elizabeth.

"Here you are dear. My, you have grown, you know. And you're looking very ladylike." She gave Elizabeth a tight squeeze. "We heard about the accident, Liz. My word! What a thing to happen. Andrew and I were shocked. Imagine our Bartholomew jumping in like that. And just for Helena's bobble."

"I know, Mrs Barlow. I don't think we've really recovered from the shock ourselves."

Mrs Barlow smiled her rosy cheeked, warm smile that could work magic.

"Don't you worry now, Lizzy. We're praying for Toby."

"Thank you. Toby's needs all your prayers. He's not doing well at all . . . anyway, Mrs Barlow, I need to buy some . . . ooh, ouch, ouch. What on earth . . . ouch . . ."

Something had nipped Elizabeth's ankle and when she looked own she saw the culprit. A tiny Labrador pup was busy licking Elizabeth's shoes.

"Hello, who's this?" Liz knelt down and lifted the puppy. The dog turned its attention to Liz's face now licking her ears and nose.

"Eh, stop it. You're tickling me."

"Peanut, come here. How did you get out" Mrs Barlow held out her hand and Elizabeth handed over her new friend.

"This is Peanut, Elizabeth. We're grandparents now!," Mrs Barlow laughed heartily. Chester and Cindy have had a litter of four puppies. They are so cute. Let's go to the shed. I'll show you."

Elizabeth followed Mrs Barlow, whispering to Tippy to remain calm.

"I love dogs now Lizzy, remember. I'm not scared anymore," Tippy whispered back.

Mrs Barlow led them to a small shed at the back of the shop. She went inside and Elizabeth followed.

"Oooooh, they're adorable," squealed Elizabeth. Cindy was lying down with the puppies climbing all over her. Peanut ran to his siblings. Elizabeth went up to the basket and stroked Cindy. The other puppies were just as friendly as Peanut and were soon competing for Liz's attention, climbing onto her lap when she sat down to stroke them.

"Where's Chester, Mrs Barlow?"

"Oh, Andrew's taken him for a walk. They should be back soon."

Elizabeth was so engrossed in the puppies' antics that she lost track of the time.

"Psst, Elizabeth", came Tippy's voice in the loudest whisper she could muster, "don't you think we should be going home?!"

"Huh? Oh gosh. I got carried away didn't I? Yes we should. Mrs Barlow, I think I should be heading home now." Mrs Barlow was outside getting some garden supplies for the shop

"Alright, love. You take care and give your mum and dad our love and Lenny too. Oh, did you need anything from the shop?"

"Yes please. I almost forgot, those puppies certainly won me over. Just some milk and bread thank you."

Elizabeth paid for the groceries and was soon on her way back to the Kowhai.

"It was so nice playing with those pups, Tippy, for a while things didn't seem so bleak and hopeless."

They were half way up the hilly path to the Kowhai.

"Can you stop walking for a minute, Lizzy?" said Tippy. "Look around you. What do you see?"

"I see a dull winter sky and lots of hills in the distance, covered in cold snow," replied Elizabeth. "Why?"

"Do you know what I see? I see the snow and the sky but to me they look beautiful. And when I look even closer I can see that beneath all the icy white lies a warm dazzling green that's hiding till spring arrives. I also see a blue sky with a sparkling sun gleaming brightly over buttercup filled fields. Summer will come, Elizabeth. Just like autumn and winter. Life is just like the seasons, Liz. It cannot always be summer. But difficult times will pass too, just like winter fades away to bring in the newness of spring."

"I know, Tippy. You're right. I do try and see things on a brighter note but now, I mean . . . what if we lost Toby."

"Elizabeth had managed to control her emotions since Toby went into hospital. She kept telling herself he would be ok. But she couldn't anymore. She had to face it, Toby wouldn't be coming back. Elizabeth sat down on a mound of grass and cried. Serendipity rested her small, delicate head against Liz's tear stained face.

"Try not to cry Liz. Just think. Amidst all this uncertainty you still managed to enjoy yourself with those puppies, didn't you. For a little while you weren't worried at all. That's how things are, Liz. Toby may die, but you will still have a treasure chest filled with memories of the most sincere, loving dog in the world. You will never lose that."

Elizabeth wiped her face. "Thank you Tippy," she said gently kissing Tippy's soft hand.

"Now, let's go home. We better get this milk to your mum before she begins to think that we've gone in search of some cows!"

# *Encore*

THERE WERE ONLY two weeks left for the Christmas holidays. The days following the accident hadn't been easy. Toby's breathing was much better now but his reduced food intake and the overall strain on his system meant that he was still very weak.

Every evening Elizabeth and Tippy visited Toby. Tippy was always the first to give Toby a kiss. He opened his eyes when Lizzy stroked his head. Toby's loud bark was reduced to a soft whimper.

"Hang in there Tobykins," said Lizzy, "We really miss you."

Primrose High was busy preparing for the talent evening. Most of the teachers had completed their portions for the winter term so there was very little class work to be done apart from the odd completion of assignments and handing out of worksheets for the holidays.

The talent show was everybody's main focus with teachers and students putting in a concerted effort to make the evening a success. The school' auditorium had a seating capacity of more than three hundred guests and a state of the art sound and lighting system. The number of entries for the event was far more than expected—there were dancers, singers, musicians, magicians and even a couple of comedians and acrobats

"I must say, I didn't think we had Hollywood, the West End and The Russian Circus all put together right here at Primrose High!" Ms Barrymore remarked during assembly.

Invitations for the night were given to all the parents. Some of the senior children were already on the lookout for university places after they completed High school. The guest list included course coordinators and teachers from colleges and universities in and around the Peak District. So the evening would be an opportunity for the students to 'get noticed' and maybe help them later on when they apply for university places.

The children were especially excited because Felicity Brown was going to be the Chief Guest. Ms Brown was a highly successful Ballet dancer who had recently been awarded 'Artiste of the Year' by the National Dance Academy. A graduate in Mathematics, Ms Brown was a role model for students who felt daunted by the prospect of having to give up their other interests and talents for the sake of a proper education.

"If Swan Lake and Algebra can go hand in hand, I'm sure anything will. It's just about determination," were Ms Brown's words when asked in an interview, if it was difficult to focus on two very different areas of study.

The children participating in the show were permitted to spend the afternoon practising either at school or at home.

Elizabeth and Mirabel spent their afternoon helping the staff with the arrangements. Mirabel was much more at ease with Elizabeth now, always enquiring about Toby and constantly reassuring Liz that he would be ok. Although Abigail joined Mirabel and Elizabeth to visit Bartholomew at the hospital, conversation between Elizabeth and Abi was strained. They avoided being together except in a group.

The evening before the concert, Liz was held up at school to help out with some last minute preparations. She was disappointed that it was too late to stop by the surgery to check on Toby.

"I'll have to go first thing in the morning, mum", she said hungrily gulping down some chicken salad. "We only need to reach school for

5 pm".

"Yes. I'm sure you'll have time. Have you finished eating, Liz? Listen, it's been a long day. If you've finished eating why don't you go and get ready for bed. You don't have to help with the washing up. Dad and I will manage."

"Will we!!!?" Dr Atkins looked up with raised eyebrows from his snug position on the sofa.

"Richard!!"

"Dad! You always get to be lazy after dinner. Tonight it's my turn," Elizabeth playfully threw a cushion at her father.

It wasn't long before Liz was cosily tucked up under her duvet. When she closed her eyes her thoughts travelled back to when she was in kindergarten. She remembered an extremely cute, chubby, five year old Easter bunny standing on a stage holding an equally cute violin. Abigail. How adorable she looked! The event in Liz's memory was the Matlock Community Easter Fair and Abigail had won the fancy dress competition. It wasn't just the fluffiness of the bunny costume that won her the prize. Abi's musical calibre was outstanding even at the tender age of five.

Whilst in Primary school, Abi's parents had been approached on a number of occasions by various television channels, with the promise of making their daughter famous overnight. But they had declined. Abigail may be a prodigy but to her parents she was first and foremost a child. And childhood only happens once. Mr and Mrs Swift feared that while the glare of the spotlight would most certainly bring her fame and fortune, Abi would lose out on the most important things. Like a sound education and good friends. Elizabeth let out an exasperated grunt!

"Elizabeth, are you awake? Are you having nightmares or are you turning into a pig! Elizabeth!!!"

"Shush, Tippy. I know you've got a soft voice but when you squeal straight into my ear it's almost painful. Now quieten down. I'm not asleep. And I am definitely not turning into a pig. I was just thinking about Abi."

Tippy kissed Elizabeth's cheek." Listen Liz, for what it's worth I think you've handled things very well."

"Thank you Tippy. I just can't stand being so uncomfortable around Abi. Yet, at the same time I don't regret telling her what I did."

"Well, then that's all that matters. I've said it before Lizzy. If your reasons for doing things are sincere and unselfish, then leave everything else to happen as it's meant to. Now try counting sheep if you're finding it difficult to fall asleep. That's bound to make you sleepy. Hey, maybe it'll improve your maths as well!! Tee hee!!" Tippy giggled.

"Tippee, shut up! You cheeky fairy, I would throw this pillow at you but the last thing I want is a squashed fairy on mum's new pillow covers."

Elizabeth didn't have to count many sheep. She was asleep before she could get to the farm! She was very restless, though, tossing and turning. The nightmare was awful. The boat had capsized and Liz was in the water; cold, deep water. There was nothing to hold on to. The water was so icy she couldn't find the strength to swim. There was water everywhere. She was sinking now, where was everyone else?

Elizabeth woke up with a start. Her face was wet! She opened her eyes to find a familiar face with large droopy eyes and a wet snout peering into hers.

"Toby! Toby, You're home. I don't understand. Oh my God!"

In his excitement on seeing his dear, sweet Lizzy, Toby had slavered Liz's face in doggy drool and woken her up.

Liz's parents were in the room now.

"We didn't want to tell you in case something went wrong. Toby was showing signs of improvement since Thursday and this morning Dr Baldwin rang to say we could pick him up," said Elizabeth's father.

"Yes, and since you've slept most of the morning away", continued her mum glancing at Liz's bedroom clock, "it was easy to keep the surprise."

"Is it that late? Oh Toby. I'm so happy, so very happy." There were tears in Liz's eyes as she hugged her favourite 'soft toy'.

"Where's Tippy? Don't tell me she's hiding. I thought she'd overcome her fear. She's just being silly now. Hey, Tippy where are you? Weren't you the one hugging Toby in hospital? What's the difference now, stop being such a sissy and come out."

"Who are you calling a sissy?" the voice was coming from Toby.

"Huh?"

Elizabeth looked at him. From behind Toby's collar came a pair of wings and a mischievous smile. Tippy had been clinging to Toby all along.

Elizabeth thought she would take Toby for a stroll before she left for school. However, her dad told her that Dr Baldwin had specifically advised that Toby would need plenty of rest and shouldn't be rushed into things. Walking would have to wait for another day. Instead, she decided to go to school a little early

"I'm sure Ms Barrymore wouldn't mind the help. There's always something to do in the last minute."

By three o clock Elizabeth was spruced up and ready to go. Except for the ones who were performing, the students were meant to be in school uniform. Elizabeth put in an extra effort to have her hair tied back neatly instead of waiting for her mum to yell after her.

"See you later everyone," Elizabeth tousled Toby's fur as she walked towards the door.

"Wait for me," Tippy flew out through an open window,

"Hey, maybe you should wait for *me*, Tippy"

"I am, slow coach."

When Liz opened the door Tippy was fluttering around in circles in front of her.

When she arrived at school, Liz saw that most of the senior classes were already there helping out. At around half past four the guests started to arrive.

"Don't they look posh," whispered Tippy

"Shush . . . Tippy. People will think I'm speaking to myself."

"Fine, spoilt sport, but they do look posh."

"Ok, now please be quiet."

By 5 'o' clock, the hall was almost full. The girls found it really difficult to tone down their 'ooh's' and 'ah's' when Felicity Brown entered the hall. She was every bit as elegant and graceful as they had imagined.

Ms Barrymore welcomed all the guests and invited Ms Brown to say a few words.

"It is an honour to be here. I want to wish all the participants the very best. I know you're nervous. So am I, believe it or not, and I'm not even performing. I assure you those nerves are quite natural. They're not a sign of weakness. In fact they show strength. They show determination. They show the desire to excel. I sincerely hope that all of you excel beyond your own expectations"

At this Elizabeth sighed. Tippy who was comfortably hidden in Elizabeth's blazer pocket popped her head out.

"What now, Liz", she asked

"Tippy I think the idea of Abigail singing is *most definitely* beyond any of our expectations."

"Yes. But if you continue to grimace and sigh and whisper to me in this fashion you're the one who is going to raise a few eyebrows.

"Ok Ok, I'll shut up"

The speeches over, the first item was now being introduced, a solo classical vocal by Alison Radcliffe. The curtain rose and Alison's voice reverberated across the auditorium, loud and crystal clear. Undoubtedly, she had a fantastic voice. Having performed on stage from a very young age, Alison performed with confidence. Alison's performance was followed by a solo ballet recital by a girl from year seven. A group of two boys and two girls performed a street dance choreographed to the latest fast tracks to hit the charts. It was a huge hit and had everyone cheering and clapping.

Then it was Abigail's turn. The moment the curtains rose, Elizabeth impulsively closed her eyes. She couldn't bear to watch Abi sing, especially after the exemplary performances the other participants had just displayed. Her heart was racing as she waited in anticipation for Abigail's voice. When the music began, though, Elizabeth's eyes opened in amazement. Abigail was on stage in a flowing black dress, with her long brown hair falling over her shoulders. She was playing her violin. Elizabeth gasped looking at Tippy. Serendipity just smiled.

The music continued. Abigail began her performance with some classical compositions and then surprised the audience by making a sudden yet smooth transition into contemporary music with motion picture soundtracks and faster pieces which immediately had the students clapping. Everyone was spellbound as the young girl masterfully blended note after note into her own compositions, a violin medley that would appeal to everyone from music maestros to school children.

Abigail, however, was oblivious of the impact she was making. Eyes closed, smiling to herself as she cradled the violin under her chin, she was in a world of her own, doing what she enjoyed most and did best!

Abigail was given a standing ovation when she finished and there were shouts of 'encore'. Elizabeth wasn't clapping though.

She was waiting backstage. Abi saw her as soon as she entered the dressing room. They looked at each other. Abi smiled. That was all that Elizabeth needed. She rushed up to Abigail and hugged her.

"Sorry"

They both said it at the same time.

"For what, Lizzy" said Abigail, "being the truest friend anyone could ever wish for?"

"I didn't want to hurt your feelings, Abi."

"Elizabeth, haven't you heard? No pain, no gain! If you hadn't been so honest, I would be out there making a complete idiot out of myself. Thank you for giving me a wakeup call."

Abigail squeezed Elizabeth's hand.

"I cherish your friendship Elizabeth. I always will."

"I treasure yours too, Abi. In fact, I feel like showing off—tonight's star performer is my best friend. You had them gobsmacked Abi. Congratulations!"

Abigail and Elizabeth felt closer to one another than they had ever felt before.

The evening was finally coming to an end. The show was a huge success and Felicity Brown personally congratulated all the children who had performed.

"You have a very bright future, Abigail, she said shaking Abi's hand. "I'm sure you've left a lasting impression on everyone who saw you perform tonight. You were simply exceptional."

As other guests approached Abi to congratulate her, Elizabeth slowly excused herself from the growing crowd of admirers.

"Tippy, I wonder where mum and dad are. Oh, there they are."

"Lizzy, wasn't Abi super duper. Where is she? I can't wait to tell her how excited I was when she did the Disney song. It was just like in the movies. Wow."

Helena was bubbly as usual.

"There she is. There she is . . . Ooh Abi. You were amazing, like someone famous."

"What do you mean 'like' Helena? After tonight's performance, I think she's already famous. In fact, she's already got a fan club right here. You were outstanding Abigail. You must be so proud, Catherine", said Mrs Atkins to Abi's mother who had joined them.

Just then Abigail let out a huge yawn.

"Oops, pardon me. Guess all the practising's got to me. I didn't realise I was so tired."

"Actually I think all of us are tired," said Dr Atkins. "It's going to be half nine. You've got the weekend to re-live the excitement. We should be heading home now."

In the car park Abigail looked at Elizabeth with teary eyes.

"Goodnight Lizzy. What would I do without you . . ."

"Oh, don't be so sentimental Abi, I'm sure you'll think of something . . . hee hee. Next time you decide to give me the silent treatment, though, could you please tell me how long it's going to last. That way I wouldn't lose any sleep over it. OUCH!"

Abigail playfully punched Elizabeth in the side.

In the car, Elizabeth was silent, gazing out at the starlit sky.

"Hmmm", she sighed with a hint of a smile.

"What's that dear? Did you say something?" Richard Atkins looked at his daughter through the rear view mirror. Elizabeth was slowly nodding off.

"She said she loves happy endings, Dr Atkins," said Tippy.

# MiSsChief Makers

THE SUN WAS shining over the hills in the Peak District. The last patches of snow melted away in its warmth. The drab lifelessness of winter had in its place the bounty and plenitude of spring—trees with new leaves, cherry blossom and buds waiting to bloom into a myriad of colours. Outside the Kowhai, another sort of competition was going on . . .

"Shoo, go away. Lizzy, help me. Shoo, stop it, Lizee!

"You asked for it Tippy. I told you to pick on someone your own size."

"I was NOT Picking on it. I thought it might want to be my pet. You know, like you and Toby."

"Oh, right. That makes sense. Pet huh? Tippy, the butterfly is definitely the same size as you if not bigger. Besides, I sincerely doubt if it understands English which means you won't be able to ask it to 'sit' like we tell Toby. In any case, I think it's giving you enough trouble already."

Elizabeth and Tippy were on their way home after Liz's maths tuition. A butterfly had taken a liking to Elizabeth's winged companion probably assuming that it had found one of its own kind. Tippy, though excited at first, was now finding it very irksome to get rid of the creature. Elizabeth was having fun watching Tippy lose balance every time the butterfly brushed its wings against hers.

"Please, Lizzy. I've had enough."

Elizabeth waved the butterfly away with a quick flick of her hand.

"What a relief!" said Tippy.

"Speaking of relief, the maths tuition is really helping, Tippy. I'm able to focus better and for a change, getting more answers right than wrong!! I guess maths isn't that bad after all."

"Good for you Liz."

They were almost at the Kowhai now after the fifteen minute walk from Mr Fletcher's Science and Mathematics Tuition centre. Mr Fletcher was a retired teacher from St Peters Grammar School. His experience and the remarkable results many of his students achieved in school and university meant that Mr Fletcher's guidance was much sought after.

When school reopened after the winter break, Ms Roberts suggested that Elizabeth may benefit from Mr Fletcher's coaching

"It might help, Elizabeth. In fact, I'm sure it will. Who knows, you may end up being our top scorer in the finals."

Elizabeth knew Ms Roberts was pulling her leg with her very optimistic prediction!

"Ms Roberts, I think pigs will have to fly before that happens!"

In any case Liz signed up for Mr Fletcher's classes. After just a few sessions with him, she realised that even if pigs couldn't fly, with a little encouragement and effort, her maths might just 'take off'!

When they got home Liz's mum opened the door.

"Hello darling. I was hoping you'd be back soon."

"Why, is something wrong, mum?"

"No, no. It's just that when I looked at my calendar I realised that I've got a meeting at work tomorrow. I don't know how I could have missed it. Anyway, I need to complete some paperwork so we're having an early tea, that's all. I want to tidy up and get cracking. Liz, why don't you help yourself to some stew? Dad and Helena have already finished. I think they're watching something on telly."

"Mum please can I eat in the living room. I promise to be careful."

Mrs Atkins gave Elizabeth a knowing smile.

"Hmm, can't bear the thought of missing out, can you? Fine. The program is supposed to be worth watching. I think it's something about African Elephants. I heard dad telling Helena about it."

Elizabeth walked into the living room with her plate. As she entered she heard Helena squeal.

"Please, Daddy. Please, please, please can Lizzy and I go? Please."

"Helena, quieten down," said Dr Atkins.

As soon as Helena caught sight of Elizabeth she started jumping up and down again.

"Lizzy, you won't believe it. MISschief's coming next month. The advertisement was on just now and she looks so cool. She's going to perform at the Pavilions in Sheffield. We'll get to watch her singing 'Destiny'. I can't wait to go."

"Hello. Hang on a minute little missy," Dr Atkins pulled Helena on to the Sofa next to him.

"SIT! I'm going to have to speak to you like I do to Toby if you don't contain your excitement a little bit. Helena, when did we decide that you'll be going to the concert? Ok you saw the advert but we still need to know more details before we can make any decisions. By the look of things, tickets are going to be expensive. So don't get too enthusiastic, just yet."

"Why don't I sing for you instead," giggled Tippy.

"Tippee!!

The girls were in no mood for Tippy's jokes. Even the boisterous antics of an African baby elephant with his siblings didn't do much to revive their deflated spirits.

"Listen you two, it's getting late. Why don't you get ready for bed, Helena? Liz will join you once she's finished eating. We can think about MISschief tomorrow . . . oops . . . hey . . . Toby!!"

Mrs Atkins almost fell over as she walked towards the settee with her plate. Toby couldn't resist the smell of chicken salad and almost tripped her over in a futile attempt to win a small piece. Disgruntled, he settled down on his rug and in no time was enjoying something he loved more than chicken—a good long snooze.

On the television screen the late evening news had taken the place of African Elephants. Christine Atkins rolled her eyes and sighed for the hundredth time at her husband's annoying habit of switching channels every now and then.

"Richard, the programme isn't over yet . . . !"

"There's only five minutes left and the girls are going to bed. So what does it matter."

That was that. Mrs Atkins wasn't bothered. Since she had work to complete she wasn't going to watch television anyway. Still, she shook her head.

"What is it with men and the news." she asked, not expecting any answer. Even though Dr Atkins was too absorbed in the headlines to pay any attention to his wife's remarks, Tippy was quick to respond.

"I've often wondered that myself, Mrs Atkins. I've come to the conclusion that maybe they have to watch it every ten minutes because they can't remember what happened in the previous bulletin! Hee, hee . . ."

"Hey, I heard that, Tippy. Just you wait . . ."

"Goodnight Dr Atkins", Tippy kissed Dr Atkins' forehead and fluttered onto Elizabeth's shoulders.

"Goodnight Dad. Goodnight mum."

A starlit sky shone down on the Kowhai. The lights inside were turned off one by one as African Elephants, dogs, girls and fairies drifted into a peaceful slumber. Beyond the horizon, the sun waited patiently, heralding a new dawn.

Primrose High was engulfed in MiSschief madness. When she arrived at school the next day, Elizabeth was greeted with at least fifteen 'Have you heard's and 'are you going's even before she entered the classroom.

Amidst all the excitement Alison Radcliffe was sat poised and snooty as ever at her desk.

"Dad's definitely going to get me a ticket for the concert. But I might not go. I'm sure I'll probably have something more important to do. Besides I've already gone to two of MiSschief's concerts anyway."

Alison sighed as she flicked open one of her books trying to look totally indifferent. As usual Abigail wanted to pounce on her! Alison's condescending attitude was simply intolerable.

"Oh I'm sure you'll find plenty of interesting things to do, Alison. Too bad you won't have anyone to keep you company."

Alison glared at Abi.

"You're just jealous Abigail," she started in a feeble hearted attempt to counter Abi's quick witted remark. Just then Ms Fitzgerald walked in.

"Good morning girls. Could I have some order please? Shush . . . , quiet now."

Ms Fitzgerald smiled looking at her class.

"Hmm, that's better. Now then, how many of you looked at the morning papers?"

Lots of hands went up immediately.

"That's jolly good. I didn't think I had so many students who liked to keep up to date with current affairs. So, how many of you actually read the headlines?"

All the hands went down.

"Ah Ha, that's more like it. I mean, after all, the *news* is only of 'secondary' importance in newspapers, isn't it! Well, at least you're all honest!"

With a twinkle in her eye, Ms Fitzgerald took out a couple of paper cuttings from her bag.

"I presume that even though you didn't have the time or inclination to read the paper, you would have managed to get one of these. The newspaper cuttings were actually entries for a competition to win two tickets to see MISsChief in concert. Most of the girls had seen the entry form and had already started filling it in.

"Girls, I understand that you must be excited beyond words," continued Ms Fitzgerald. However, it's important that you leave your 'MISschievous' activities for break time or after school. I do not want any distractions during class time. Do I make myself clear?"

"Yes, Ms Fitzgerald", the girls chorused.

Elizabeth made up her mind to get hold of one of the competition entry forms as soon as she got home. She'd give it a shot. There was no harm trying.

That evening, Mrs Atkins came home later than usual.

"Tied up at work, Chris?" enquired Liz's dad.

"Lots of new office and class room supplies were delivered this morning, Richard. We weren't expecting them till next month. So everything is in a bit of a muddle. Tina and Sharon said they'll come in early tomorrow to help get things in order. Oh! Thank you, darling."

Elizabeth had made her mum a cup of tea. Mrs Atkins sipped it down hungrily.

"Umm, that's lovely Lizzy. It's been a long day. How was school?"

"School was fine mum. That reminds me, Dad, have you seen today's news paper?"

Dr Atkins looked at her daughter with raised eyebrows. This was beginning to sound interesting.

"Yes, Dr Atkins. Liz has suddenly developed a keen interest in gauging as much information as she can about current trends in pop music." Tippy was ready to tease Elizabeth, as usual.

"Right, Tippy, if I win the competition you are definitely not coming with me."

"Oh come on Lizzy. I'm just having a bit of fun at your expense."

Helena giggled. Elizabeth couldn't help smiling. She had a proven track record of NOT keeping up to date with current affairs even though her parents made it a point to constantly remind her that being aware of it was just as important as learning history or science.

"Elizabeth," said Dr Atkins, "we know *exactly* how much you enjoy reading the papers so, why the sudden interest?"

Elizabeth told her parents about the competition.

"Oh, I see. Listen, Liz." Liz's mum sat down next to Elizabeth.

"It's all very well to enter a competition. But consider the chances of actually winning. Thousands of people read the paper. You might win, but what's the guarantee. I have a better idea. How about you pay for the tickets yourself?"

"Huh? You're going to buy us tickets for the concert? Oh wow, mum, that's simply . . ."

"Hey, wait a minute sweetheart. I didn't say anything of the sort." Mrs Atkins stopped Elizabeth mid sentence.

"But you . . ." Liz's mum put her hand over Elizabeth's mouth.

"Shush . . . , I know you're excited. But keep quiet for a moment and listen. I said *you* can pay for the tickets yourself, using your own money. Not Dad's or mine.

"Mum, you're not making any sense. Have I won the lottery or something", Elizabeth was mystified.

"No sweetheart, unfortunately it's not as good as that! You know, those new lot of classroom supplies I mentioned, I'm going to need help to sort them out. We were planning on hiring one or two part time staff from the agency. Instead of doing that, you and Abi could spend a few hours helping out every week or during the weekends. In two months, you'll have enough of your own hard earned money to pay for the tickets."

Elizabeth was silent for a few minutes.

"Gosh, mum. I think that's a fantastic idea. I'm sure Abi'll be happy too. Oh wow. This is simply great".

Elizabeth was thrilled to bits. The next day Liz and Abigail spent their break time working out a schedule which would enable them to fit in school work along with Mrs Atkins's attractive 'employment opportunity.'

"I think Saturday afternoon would be best too, Lizzy", said Abigail as the two girls sat down for lunch.

"Best for what?" it was Mirabel.

Abi told her about the Mrs Atkins's idea.

"Hey, where were you yesterday, Mirabel. We were all talking about the concert but we couldn't find you anywhere. Didn't you come to school?"

Mirabel looked as if she'd been caught off guard.

"I couldn't come in yesterday because I had to take my sister to the dentist. She refused to go without me. You know what a fusspot she can be, Liz, don't you?

"So, will you be going to the concert", Abigail persisted with her line of questioning.

"Actually my Dad's coming home that Friday. I'm sure he'll have something planned for us. It's almost four months now since we saw him. I can't wait."

"But surely you must want to watch MISschief. I mean, your dad won't mind, will he?"

Abigail was baffled by Mirabel's complete lack of interest. Most of the girls she knew would give an arm and a leg just to get a glimpse of MISschief in person, let alone watch her on stage. But Mirabel couldn't care less!

Elizabeth sensed what the real reason for Mirabel's attitude was. Having spent time at Mirabel's home, Liz knew that although Mirabel's family was lavish in serving out warmth and generosity, their lifestyle was anything *but* lavish. Probably by telling everyone that she would be busy on the night of the concert Mirabel was trying to evade the real reason—when every single penny counted, an expensive ticket to watch a celebrity performance was simply not a priority.

Later, Elizabeth ran her thoughts past Abigail so that she wouldn't press Mirabel too much on the matter.

"You're right, Liz. Oh no. I never meant to make Mirabel feel awkward. I just got so carried away with the whole thing"

Elizabeth nodded.

"In any case, don't beat yourself up over it. I'm sure Mirabel is far too sensible to really be affected by any of this."

""Still, we needn't 'rub it in' by being too excited in front of her. Anyway, we can't compete with Alison Radcliffe in the 'showing off' and 'rubbing it in' side of things."

Elizabeth started to giggle.

"Yeah, talk about wasted effort. When will Alison realise that the only thing astonishing about her is her thick skin! She just doesn't get it."

The girls picked up their bags and made their way to the main door. Alison Radcliffe whizzed past them.

"Catching the school bus are you? Well, I must rush. My dad sent the chauffeur early today because we're having a garden party for some of my parents' friends. See ya."

Alison ran off unaware that her skirt was bunched up from behind exposing a rather large hole in her tights. She was gone before Abi and Elizabeth had a chance to tell her that she wasn't looking as glamorous as she thought. The girls looked at one another and burst out laughing.

"I guess Alison does have a purpose. Comic relief," said Abigail as they boarded the bus. They were soon on their way home

# Change of Plans

"MY GOODNESS, SOMEBODY'S really into time management these days! I can't believe my absent minded daughter is actually trying to be more organised."

Dr Atkins was going through his paperwork, a weekend chore which he did religiously. Elizabeth was frantically jotting down items on her 'to do' list.

"I'm an earning member of the family just like you, Dad. Besides, with exams coming up, Maths tuition, working at the nursery and, of course, my usual household chores, I dare say I have much more work than you."

Dr Atkins laughed.

"It's amazing what the thought of having a little bit of money can do to people. Isn't that right, Tippy?"

Tippy was fluttering around trying to wake Toby up from his usual, *unnecessary* morning nap. She flew on to the table and peered at Liz's list.

"I agree Dr Atkins. Hmm . . . let's see. Item no 1 on the list says 'remind mum to mend hole in gym knickers'. So by 'household chores' you mean making sure that everyone else does theirs."

"Oh stop it!"

"We're just kidding, sweetheart. It's great that you're prioritizing things."

Elizabeth grinned.

"I know. I think it's great too. I've suddenly realised that there is actually so much you *can* do in 24 hours."

She put on her cardigan

"See you later. Better get to the nursery."

Elizabeth kissed her dad and was out of the door with Tippy perched on her shoulders. Toby snorted and let out a mighty sneeze. Tippy clapped.

"Yippee. It worked. I managed to wake him up with some fairy dust. Just a wee bit sprinkled on the nose, works every time."

"Tippeeee! How could you, poor Toby. If he wasn't such a good natured dog, Tippy, you would BE fairy dust now."

"Well, it's for his own good. He sleeps too much anyway. It's not healthy."

"Ok, Doctor. You've made your point. Now let's speed up."

Elizabeth and Abigail had already spent a good few hours helping out Mrs. Atkins. Books, Toys, Pencils, Papers—everything was sorted, put in boxes and labelled appropriately.

"Not bad, girls, not bad at all," Liz's mum looked approvingly at what the girls had done. "Maybe you should become permanent staff here, on second thoughts, maybe not. I doubt if you'd be this efficient if a couple of concert tickets weren't in the bargain!"

"Mum, how can you say that? I would help you anytime. All you have to do is ask . . ."

Mrs Atkins gave Liz a playful shove. Elizabeth smiled cheekily. Whether their hard work was motivated by the goodness of their hearts or the desire to join hundreds of other screaming MISschief fans, at the end of four weeks the girls were delighted to accept their pay check from an equally delighted Mrs Atkins. They rushed into town to purchase their tickets.

That night as she lay in bed, Elizabeth gazed down at Tippy adjusting the cotton wool in her shoe box.

"Tippy, when you do things for others it makes you feel—well, actually I can't even describe what it feels like . . . happy. No, happier than happy . . . content. Yes, that's what it is, content—perfectly happy and content."

"Gosh, if helping your mum makes you so "perfectly happy', why don't you do it more often."

"No, no. I'm not talking about mum."

"What do you mean? Who else have you been working for?"

"No one, Tippy, it's not work. It's, uh, nothing. Now go to sleep Tippy."

"Yes, I think I will. You're not making any sense Elizabeth. Good night."

"Goodnight"

Liz rolled over and closed her eyes. "It makes a lot of sense to me, Tippy' she thought.

In her shoe box, Tippy smiled. She knew exactly what was going through Liz's head. Elizabeth was growing up, growing up with her heart in the right place.

Serendipity the fairy felt 'perfectly happy' too . . .

With only a week left till the concert teachers at primrose high were finding it almost impossible to contain the girls' excitement and get them to focus on their work.

"There are still five more days left, girls. Don't let your excitement get the better of you," said Ms Fitzgerald handing out some grammar exercises. "MISschief is going to sing and dance her way into the future—quite literally. You girls might be doing that in a few years time, but for now you have to get through high school."

The girls handed in their work when the bell rang for lunch hour.

"Liz, I'm just going to speak to Ms Dawson about my School Bus Money. Mum's been after me at least a million times."

"That's fine Abi. I need to speak to Mirabel anyway."

The girls parted and Elizabeth looked around for Mirabel.

"That's funny. She was right here a minute ago," thought Elizabeth, "I told her we'd meet for lunch."

Elizabeth proceeded towards the dinner hall, assuming that Mirabel must have gone first to grab a place for both of them. But there was no sign of her there either. As Elizabeth turned to go and ask some of the other girls if they'd seen Mirabel, she caught sight of her speaking to Ms Fitzgerald. They were standing quite a distance away from Elizabeth. Mirabel was facing the other way so she didn't see Elizabeth. Liz waited expecting Mirabel to turn around as soon as the conversation was over. Surprisingly, that wasn't what happened. Ms Fitzgerald hugged Mirabel and gave her a pat on the back.

Elizabeth wondered what Mirabel had done. Ms Fitzgerald was certainly pleased with her. Maybe she'd got another A on her assignment. Liz watched eagerly. She couldn't wait to congratulate Mirabel. But instead of walking towards the dinner hall, Mirabel headed towards the school's main door.

"Wow, this must be really good news, if Mirabel is going home to tell her mum', thought Liz. She ran after Mirabel hastily.

"Mirabel wait. Where are you going? Wait. I've got a surprise for you, Mirabel . . ."

Mirabel's pace hastened. Elizabeth was baffled. Why was Mirabel behaving like this?

"Mirabel, STOP!" Elizabeth summoned up all her strength and ran as fast as she could. Mirabel was only an arm's length away now.

"Mirabel, why won't you stop? It's just me."

Mirabel turned to face Elizabeth.

"Mirabel, what's wrong. Oh no! Are you ill?"

Mirabel's eyes were red and face tear stained.

"Liz, I didn't want you to see me like this. I'm alright, really."

"Mirabel, of course you're not alright. Come here."

Elizabeth took Mirabel's hand and both the girls sat down on a nearby bench.

"Aren't you feeling well? Would you like me to come home with you? I'm sure Ms Fitzgerald won't mind."

Mirabel shook her head.

"No, Liz. I'm fine, just a bit upset."

"I can see that, but why? Please tell me, Mirabel. I hate to see you cry like this."

"I'm too embarrassed. It's quite silly actually."

Elizabeth sighed.

"Listen, Mirabel. I am your friend. Nothing that upsets you would be 'silly' for me. Now come on. What's wrong?"

Mirabel looked at Elizabeth fighting back tears.

"It's my dad. He won't be able to come home for another couple of months. I miss him so much, Liz. It's not easy not having him around you know. Oh! I shouldn't complain. Sorry. You probably think I'm really ungrateful, sobbing about things like this, Silly me. Anyway . . ."

Mirabel couldn't complete the sentence. Elizabeth hugged her as tight as she could.

"Well, now we're both silly."

Elizabeth didn't cry easily. But she found the sincerity and disappointment in Mirabel's voice so moving that she couldn't fight back the tears. Mirabel smiled.

"Don't we look a sight? Good thing everyone's in the dinner hall. Listen, Liz why don't you carry on and have lunch. I'll see you tomorrow. I need to go home early because Robbie is tied up at college and I need to get mum some things which can't wait till after school." Mirabel wiped her face with a handkerchief.

"Oh, I almost forgot. What's this surprise you've got to tell me? Have you won an art contest?"

Elizabeth opened her school bag.

"Mirabel, I hope you won't mind. I wanted to give this to you. I thought that your Dad surely wouldn't have a problem with you staying away for one evening."

Elizabeth handed over an envelope to Mirabel.

"What is it, Liz?"

"Open it Mirabel."

Puzzled, Mirabel opened the envelope.

"My word, Elizabeth, I couldn't! It's too much. This is too much Elizabeth. Thank you. But I absolutely refuse. You've been looking forward to it for so long. I really don't care if I can't go Lizzy. Please, Liz. I can't accept this. It's very good of you, but I just can't."

Mirabel was so surprised at Elizabeth's gesture she wouldn't stop shaking her head.

"You're so generous."

"Listen, I will have other chances to go and I know that with all the things you have to worry about, watching MISschief isn't top of the list. Mirabel, I'm very sorry your dad can't come home as planned. But at least you can enjoy the evening."

Mirabel was still shaking her head.

"You're an angel, Elizabeth. I don't know what to say."

"Just say that you'll go. It would make me extremely happy if you went, so stop being so stubborn!" Elizabeth smiled and hugged Mirabel. "I've got to get back to class so I'll leave you two alone now. You better make the right choice."

"What do you mean 'you *two?*'"

"You and the ticket, it's definitely not coming back with me. See ya."

Elizabeth ran off leaving Mirabel alone on the bench staring at the precious piece of paper in her hand.

A little fairy fluttered overhead. Nobody saw her. Nobody saw the smile on her tiny face. Serendipity flew over the trees and the hills back to the Kowhai. What would everyone say to Liz's '*slight*' change of plans? Tippy didn't have to wait long to find out.

"You did WHAT!!!!? My God, Liz, I can't believe this. We were together the whole day and you didn't breathe a word."

Abigail had come to the Kowhai for tea. She almost choked on her soup when Elizabeth revealed her 'Good Deed' for the day!

"Sorry, Abi, I was a bit nervous about how you'd react. I mean we've both been planning this for months. I didn't want to let you down but at the same time I really needed to do this for Mirabel. Please try to understand."

Toby nuzzled against Elizabeth's legs whilst she waited silently for Abigal to speak

"Liz, I am disappointed that you won't be coming. But you haven't let me down. No way. In fact, gosh, I think it's great, Liz, really great. I'm sure Mirabel must be very *very* happy."

Elizabeth giggled.

"She's more than happy, I think. I left her quite dumbfounded! Blabbering on about how she just couldn't accept the ticket. Anyway, I hope the thought of going to the concert will cheer her up. I caught her in tears this afternoon. Apparently, her dad won't be coming home as planned."

Mrs Atkins walked over to Elizabeth and kissed her. She didn't say anything. There was no need to say anything. The silence that accompanied the kiss said it all. Christine Atkins was proud of her daughter.

"What about me, Liz. Will I have to go without you?" Helena looked up at Elizabeth pleadingly. She wasn't happy. This certainly wasn't part of the plan. Ok, fine. It's wonderful to help someone out and all that. But hey, going to the concert without Elizabeth was unthinkable.

"My, my, do I see some sisterly affection seeping in?" said Dr Atkins giving Helena a playful nudge. "Actually, we've got our own little surprise for you. We're paying for your tickets. So you can all go, you too Abi. It's our treat"

"Wow, thanks Dad." Elizabeth leaned over and kissed her mum who was sitting next to her. "You too mum, you're the best. Hopefully, Mirabel won't have any problem accepting the ticket now. She didn't want me to lose out because of her. That's not a reason anymore."

Abigail got up from her seat at the table and went round and hugged Elizabeth's parents.

"Thanks a lot. I just want you to know that I'll be happy to work for you anytime, seeing as its *soooooooo well paid*!"

"Don't push your luck, Abi. This is just the one off. Next time you'll have to treat *us* to a concert."

Bartholomew whimpered. He went up to Dr Atkins and held out his paw.

"What about me?" said his doleful eyes.

"Ok boy. You want some attention as well don't you? Don't worry. We'll make you an extra special meal when the girls go to the concert."

Dr Atkins patted Toby and ruffled up his coat. It was just what Toby wanted. Reassurance that he was still very important, that his tummy was *even more important* and that silly pop stars were not going to get in the way!!

That night as she snuggled down under the bedcovers, Elizabeth couldn't wipe the smile off her face.

."Yes, it's a wonderful feeling isn't it when you make someone happy, especially someone like Mirabel. Goodnight Tippy.

"Goodnight, Liz."

# MISsChief's
# Magnificent Mischief

IT WAS SATURDAY night—*The* Saturday night—the night that the young girls, and quite a few young guys, in the Peak District had been waiting for. *MisSchief Night*.

Elizabeth was putting on a new top and a pair of jeans that she'd bought especially for the concert. Mrs Atkins was combing Helena's hair.

"Listen, Liz. We want you to have a good time, but don't get carried away. Helena's with you too. You must take care to stay together. Don't forget your mobile phone."

"Wow, Dr Atkins . . . don't you look stylish!! Dressed to impress the girls are we?"

Liz's father came into the girls' room. He was wearing a beige blazer with a pale green shirt and new tie.

"Definitely, Tippy, so are the girls impressed?"

The 'girls' gave Dr Atkins the thumbs up.

"You do look charming, Dr Atkins."

Elizabeth's mum kissed her husband. Dr Atkins put his arms around her.

"You don't look too bad yourself, Mrs Atkins."

Elizabeth rolled her eyes and she and Helena suddenly went into a coughing fit!

"Girls, stop it! Your mum and I are entitled to our moments, you know . . ."

"We know you are, Prince Charming. That's why you're going out for a candle lit dinner in a posh restaurant—without us! So please could you save the romance for later. By the way, Dad, you can take us to Reggies' next weekend, since you're so disappointed that we can't join you tonight."

"Excuse me!! I never said anything of the . . ."

Elizabeth cut in before her father could complete his sentence.

"Gosh, would you look at the time. It's six already. We better make a move don't you think, mum. Oh, sorry dad. Were you going to say something?! Hee hee."

Elizabeth and Helena gave each other a high five. Dr Atkins reluctantly conceded victory and asked Helena to pass him the car keys from the dining table.

"Your Chauffeur is at your service, my ladies," he said bowing. The girls giggled. Their dad was such a softie.

They picked Abigail up and were soon on their way to the Grand pavilions Arena where MISschief would be performing for three successive nights. The complex had three separate theatres which could each hold up to two thousand people.

The roads weren't too busy and Liz's dad managed to get to the Arena a good half an hour before the show was due to begin.

"Ok girls. Enjoy yourselves"

"You too, love birds!!" teased Elizabeth.

As her parents left, Elizabeth saw Mirabel and Robbie at the main entrance. The girls waved at her.

"Mirabel, over here", screamed Abi. But her voice couldn't be heard over the din in the concert hall. Luckily, in spite of the throng of MiSschief fans, she still managed to get their attention. Mirabel and Robbie saw some sort of Mexican wave occurring not far from them.

"What's that?" said Robbie.

The girls' hands were flying about wildly, desperate to get noticed.

"Robbie, it's Elizabeth and Abi."

Mirabel waved to them.

"Doesn't she look thrilled, Liz?" whispered Tippy into Liz's ear. Serendipity had managed to squeeze into a fold in Elizabeth's scarf. "I've got the best seat in the Arena, Liz. Great view, don't have to move to let anyone through and it's extremely comfortable! Just make sure you don't adjust your scarf!"

They were all seated and waiting expectantly for the curtains to rise. Helena tugged at Elizabeth's blouse.

"Liz, my heart's beating so fast."

"Lenny, it's just the excitement. The show is about to . . ."

She couldn't complete her sentence. The lights went off and a man's voice boomed over the loudspeaker.

"Good evening girls and boys, or should I say 'MISschief Makers'?"

Serendipity tickled Liz's ears with her wings.

"He forgot to mention fairies . . . !"

"Shut up, Tippy."

The announcement continued with shrieks of delight resonating in the background.

"It is time. Get ready to swing your hips to your favourite tunes. Hold on to your seats coz you're definitely going to feel the vibration, because she is groovy and she is glamorous. She is only fifteen years old but has more than a million fans worldwide. She, girls and boys, is the one and only—MISschief!!!!"

With the last two words a multicoloured array of lights dazzled around the hall and the curtains rose to reveal an empty stage. There were puzzled expressions everywhere. What was going on? Suddenly, there was a loud shudder and the stage was enveloped in coloured smoke. When the cloudiness in front of their eyes cleared, the stage was no longer empty. There, surrounded by her supporting dancers stood Alicia Robinson, aka, MiSschief—the Canadian pop princess. She was wearing a sparkly golden top with a tight skirt. Her trademark long, black curls were flowing loosely around her face. The show was on!

MISschief's performance was tantalising. The girls enjoyed every song and danced to every beat. Mirabel surprised them with how 'in tune' she actually was with the pop scene. She even danced well.

"OOOH groovy, Mirabel. I didn't think you had it in you,"

Mirabel laughed.

"Neither did I. Just goes to show how comfortable you guys make me feel."

Liz looked at Abi who was screaming at the top of her voice. This wasn't a talent show after all and Abi was enjoying singing every note, even if they were slightly off key!!

"Are you sure, Mirabel?! Coz right now, I'm not feeling too comfortable."

What a magical evening it was! Unfortunately, even magical evenings do have to come to an end. With the music, singing and thunderous applause still reverberating in their ears, the girls waited near the main entrance for Dr Atkins. Mirabel and Liz stood near the door, whilst Abi sat down with Helena who was beginning to nod off.

"Thank you, Liz. It was amazing!"

Elizabeth squeezed Mirabel's hand.

"You are most welcome, Mirabel. Now no more thanking me, understand." Elizabeth frowned. "Oh, no. It's back to the books now—exams, projects . . . Oh well, at least we've got Ms Fitzgerald's send off to look forward to. Mirabel have you . . . Mirabel?"

Mirabel wasn't listening to Liz. Her eyes were staring at a figure that was approaching the building from the car park. "Mirabel, what is it?" Elizabeth felt alarmed when she saw that Mirabel's eyes were as wide as saucers, as though in shock. The man started walking towards them. It wasn't Robbie. Liz was beginning to panic.

"Mirabel, what's wrong. Who is he?"

All of a sudden Mirabel ran towards the man whose arms were now wide-open. He lifted Mirabel up and both of them were locked in a tight embrace. Elizabeth was utterly confused.

"Hmm, who could that be?" Tippy enquired, still nestling between the soft fibres of Liz's scarf. Liz didn't have time to respond. Someone tapped her shoulder.

"Hello, Elizabeth". It was Robbie.

"Robbie, you're here?! But who is Mirabel . . . What's going on?"

Liz looked around. She couldn't find Mirabel.

"I'm here, Liz". Mirabel was behind Liz. The tall man, who was previously just a shape in the dark, was now standing next to Elizabeth. He certainly was no longer a shadow. Looking at his tall, well built physique, dark eyes, and a smile that looked very familiar, it didn't take long for Elizabeth to fit the pieces together.

"You're Mirabel's father, aren't you?"

"You're spot on, my dear. I am Mirabel's father indeed. And I am thrilled to be able to finally meet the young lady that *my* young lady speaks so highly of."

"Oh no, not at all, I mean, yes. I am so delighted to meet you too, sir. Gosh, I'm blabbering aren't I? It's just such a surprise. Mirabel you said . . ."

Mirabel shook her head. I didn't have a clue, Liz. I still can't believe this is happening. Daddy, what are you doing here? Robbie, did you know?"

Mr Mitchell laughed—a loud, hearty laugh. His daughter's astonishment and elation made all the travelling and days away from home worthwhile. There were some things in life you just couldn't put a price on.

"I'll answer all your questions on the way home. It is rather late and you should all be getting home, especially little Miss MiSschief right here."

Helena and Abi were with them now curious to see who this stranger was. Mr Mitchell patted Helena's head. He was such a jovial person. In the few minutes they spent together, Mirabel's father made Elizabeth feel as though she had known him for years. It was obvious how much he had missed Mirabel. Even as he teased Helena he had one arm tightly fastened around Mirabel's waist.

"Daddy", Helena spotted Dr Atkins walking towards them briskly with an anxious expression. Who was this tall man? Why was he speaking to the girls? Dr Atkins's agitation was somewhat eased by Helena's smile as she ran towards him. A handshake later, Dr Atkins was smiling too.

The much awaited evening was coming to an end. The girls said goodnight to one another and Elizabeth began to follow Dr Atkins to the car park. Mirabel and her dad were headed in the opposite direction. Elizabeth was almost near the car when someone tugged at her shirt.

"Liz wait," it was Mirabel.

"What is it, Mirabel? Have you forgotten something?"

Mirabel hugged Liz so tight she found it difficult to breathe.

"Elizabeth, you'll never know how much this meant to me."

Mirabel squeezed Elizabeth's hands and ran off to her Dad.

"Come on, Liz. Your mum is waiting in the car. You can talk about things in school tomorrow." Dr Atkins impatiently beckoned Elizabeth assuming that she and Mirabel were still discussing the concert.

"I don't understand some people. Always hurry, hurry, hurry. I mean what's the point of having any time if you can't spare a moment or two for the most important things—a moment for a heartfelt thanks, a moment for a few tears of joy, a moment to show your love. That's all it takes; three tiny little moments to make the millions of other moments worth living. Oh Dr Atkins, how much you miss!"

"Tippy! That's my father you're talking about and he's the best Dad in the whole world," retorted Elizabeth.

"Oooh . . . someone's rather touchy! I know he is Liz. All I meant is that Dr Atkins missed something very special because he was so intent on getting to the car. The car is not going anywhere, but that moment has passed. The best things in life do come free, Liz, you just need to pause for a moment and experience them."

"Well, Little Miss Wisdom, he puts up with all your cheeky whims so you better be nice to him, or else!"

Serendipity flew onto Dr Atkins head and started ruffling his hair with her wings.

"Of course I'll be nice to him. He's such a cuddly wuddly . . ."

"Tippy get off me. Stop it. Liz what were you talking about. Why won't Tippy be nice to me? Oh Forget it. I can't be bothered. Get in the car, please, and Tippy stop tickling my ears. We've got to get a move on."

Tippy winked at Elizabeth.

"See, we've *got to get a move on*!"

"Shut up, Tippy," smiled Elizabeth. Her voice was almost a whisper now. They'd almost forgotten that Abigail was still with them and the last thing they needed was for Abi to notice an Unidentified Flying Object right there in the car with them!

"Settle down or Abi will wonder what's going on. It's a good thing she's on the other side. Move up Helena. You don't need the whole seat. Abi could you please help Lenny shift her bottom. It seems to be stuck."

Bottoms adjusted and fairies temporarily silenced, the car moved off. What a night it had been. After all the excitement and anticipation of seeing MISschief perform, Elizabeth was surprised that she wasn't thinking about the concert at all. She was thinking of Mirabel, smiling her lovely smile. Elizabeth felt a tint of pride knowing that earlier that evening Mirabel had smiled that special smile all because of her.

# Walls Do Have Ears

It was early June and the countryside looked as though someone had brought down a rainbow and spread it out over the hill tops. Summer was Natures own beauty pageant with every single plant competing for the crown.

The creeper hanging over the entrance to Primrose High was also in full bloom. The school was now a 'MiSschief free' zone and the children were busy preparing for the year end exams and assignments. Elizabeth was in the library reading a letter which she'd already read almost five times.

After the concert Mirabel had returned to school with the news that her dad wouldn't have to be away from home so much anymore. The bad news was that the new job meant a transfer to South Wales for the whole family.

"I'm going to miss you guys. Things are happening too fast, "Mirabel told Elizabeth tearfully.

"Mirabel, it's not like you'll be moving to a different country. Anyway, you'll make plenty of new friends."

"Yeah, I guess"

It was still extremely difficult to say goodbye and the two friends clung to each other for ages before Elizabeth finally managed to wipe her eyes.

"I'll never forget you, Mirabel, never."

Mirabel couldn't say much at all. She silently held Elizabeth's hand.

"Thank you," she whispered, "for being my friend."

Every single word in the letter she was holding, reminded Elizabeth of Mirabel's genuine warmth.

"Hi Liz, what are you doing?"

Elizabeth's trance was interrupted when Abi came in. Abigail pulled up a chair next to Elizabeth.

"It's a letter from Mirabel, she sends her love, Abi. They've arrived in Cardiff and apparently her dad's new job means that they all get to be together. Mr Mitchell doesn't have to travel. She says the new school is really good too."

"I'm so happy for her, Liz, for all of them in fact. Has she . . ."

Abigail stopped mid sentence. There was a loud thud in the adjacent room which made the girls jump. They turned to see Alison Radcliffe picking up a pile of books which had fallen off the librarian, Mrs Booth's, desk.

"I guess I shouldn't be carrying so many books all at once."

"Yes. You shouldn't Alison. And probably if you returned them on time you wouldn't have to trudge around with such a truckload."

Alison immediately defended herself.

"Well, I just got back from the Lake District, Mrs Booth. We always go there this time of year and I simply can't do any work when I'm on holiday. That's the only reason why the books are slightly overdue."

Mrs Booth sighed.

"My dear Alison, I am well aware that you go on holidays ever so often. That's nice. However, whether it's to the Lake District or Zimbabwe, I expect your next set of books to be returned promptly."

Alison glared back at Mrs Booth.

"Yes, Mrs Booth," she said defiantly.

Mrs Booth couldn't care less. She had been the school librarian for more than fifteen years and knew girls like Alison Radcliffe through and through. The less importance you gave them the better. Whether it was the Queen of England, the Princess of Persia or Primrose High's very own Little Miss Splendid, rules were rules and Mrs Booth was not about to bend them.

Liz and Abigail watched Alison fume past them.

"Mrs Booth is such a sourpuss anyway," remarked Alison to Chloe and Michelle. Alison's two ardent devotees were as always sympathetic to her 'plight'.

"Imagine calling Mrs Booth a sourpuss," said Abigail. "She's one of the most amicable people I know. Anyway, what are you revising?"

Abigail glanced over and noticed that Elizabeth had her Maths textbook open.

"Oh yes, I was meaning to ask you. How are you doing with the maths papers, Liz?"

Elizabeth opened her maths workbook.

"Ta da . . ."

"Wow, Liz. Not bad. Not bad at all. Imagine that, you've managed to get an A. You must be pleased."

Elizabeth smiled.

"'Surprised' is a more accurate a word. I don't know how this happened, Abi, but I actually enjoy tackling maths problems now. Going to Mr Fletcher has definitely helped. I suppose I'd just told myself that I couldn't do it. Now it's the reverse. Every time I get a correct answer I feel more convinced that I can do it after all."

Abi giggled.

"You sound like Dr Domingo on Life TV's 'Mind, body and soul.'"

Abigail put on a false voice.

"Just speak to your true inner self. Don't let your mind hold you back. Let it convince you that you can do it after all . . ."

"Oh stop it Abi. I don't know about my *mind, body and soul* but my Maths is definitely improving and I'm not going to give up."

"I was just kidding Liz. Good for you." Abi passed Liz her work book when the bell rang for Ms Fitzgerald's lesson.

"Abi, Ms Fitzgerald's send off is week after next isn't it? Have you decided what you're going to get her?"

"I've thought of a couple of things. She loved those orchids at 'The Sahara'. I might get her some for her greenhouse. Either that or a book about gardening, but then I'm sure Ms Fitzgerald's probably got plenty of those."

"Actually I'm thinking of getting her a book too, about India. I remember Ms Fitzgerald telling us how she's always had a fascination for India—'Gardening and India, my two passions.'

Abi smiled thinking of Ms Fitzgerald, all dreamy-eyed, describing the Taj Mahal to her class after a visit to India.

"So have you decided which book?" she asked.

"I asked Mrs Booth if she had any books to recommend and she was very helpful, especially when I told her who it was for. The book is called 'An Indian Adventure'. It's by an Indian author with a really long name. I can't pronounce it, so I've written it down.

The girls quickened their pace not wanting to be late for their lesson. Behind them, Alison Radcliffe slowed down. She didn't want them to notice her. She didn't want them to know that walls do have ears—very sharp ears. Well, it wasn't her fault. Elizabeth and Abigail were such blabber mouths they had no clue how loud they were. How could they when they were too busy choosing precious gifts for their precious teacher. 'An Indian Adventure,' eh! Alison had planned an adventure of her own and couldn't wait to tell Chloe and Michelle about her 'bright' idea. Well, she'd have to wait till after class. English, what a waste of time . . .

Alison was probably the only girl who considered Ms Fitzgerald's class a waste of time. For the others it topped their list of favourite subjects. This wasn't because of their love of Wordsworth or Shakespeare. It was because of Ms Fitzgerald's ability to engage their interest in a way that not many others teachers could.

"Don't assume that a topic won't interest you just because it seems ancient. If you look at it closely you'll realise that 'history' is not really that long ago. Try putting Romeo and Juliet or even a Macbeth into a lead role in one of the movies you watched recently. They'll probably suit the role better than the actual actor. Ok. Their English may be a bit peculiar and they wore funny clothes. But the story line—love, hate, revenge, deceit—that's not history. That's life."

And *that* was Ms Fitzgerald. Whatever the topic, her classes were full of humour and interaction that students could relate to the characters and concepts with ease.

"Ok Girls, our class is over. We'll have revision all of next week. You must practice grammar and literature over the weekend. Remember you will have choices in the exam, which is good news. However, it means that you have to be extra thorough in at least three of the prescribed textbooks. Good luck with the preparation but don't forget to enjoy the weekend."

Ms Fitzgerald felt a sudden wave of nostalgia as she left the class. It was over. Twenty five years. It didn't seem so long ago that she walked through those large doors for the first time. She almost wished she didn't have to leave.

She was about to go to the teachers cafe for a cup of coffee when Ms Fitzgerald realised that she had left an important letter for Ms Barrymore in her office. Her office was just opposite the girls' locker room. A few of the girls from Liz's class were coming out with their bags ready to go home.

"Shush . . . good thing Ms Fitzgerald's gone to the cafe. I wouldn't want her to know."

Ms Fitzgerald was about to turn the key to her office when she heard her name mentioned. She almost turned and said 'want me to know what', but then checked herself, when she heard Elizabeth's name being mentioned.

"Anyway Elizabeth Atkins is such a teacher's pet. She can't always get the credit. Little Miss perfect."

Ms Fitzgerald recognised the voice, Alison. But she was taken aback by the tone in which the words were spoken. Why such resentment. Ms Fitzgerald knew her girls had their differences in opinion. This was more than that, though. What was going on? She stood still.

"The book is supposed to be the ideal gift for Ms Fitzgerald. I heard Elizabeth telling Abigail about it. But why should Liz be the one giving it to her!!?"

Alison's scheming voice continued,

"I'm going to give Ms Fitzgerald the book before Elizabeth. In fact I'll give it to her earlier than the rest of the class. That'll make it seem extra special. So, do you think it's a good idea?"

Ms Fitzgerald hastily entered her office. She had heard enough and she didn't want the girls to notice her. She sat down at her desk with a sigh. Is that all Alison? I thought you were scheming to get Liz expelled. Good grief. My dear Alison, when will you grow up? It's going to take a lot more than a book to make me change my opinion about you. And nothing, *absolutely nothing*, will make me change what I feel for Elizabeth."

Ms Fitzgerald picked up the letter for Ms Barrymore and went in search of a really hot cup of coffee.

# *And the Plot Thickens . . .*

"YES, THEY HAVE expanded haven't they? I haven't come here for more than a year now. Gosh! It's huge!"

Elizabeth looked at Abigail who was gazing up at the numerous shelves lining the second floor. The girls were at 'A Few Words and More', a bookstore and library in Matlock Town Centre. The shop had recently renovated its 65 year old building and now boasted of two floors of books with a complete section of children's' literature.

"I know," nodded Abigail, "they should probably call it a 'few words and *a lot* more' now.

The girls were at the shop to enquire if the book that Liz wanted for Ms Fitzgerald was available. They managed to speak to one of the shop assistants.

"Oh, you're in luck," said the lady. "I'm not much of a history person myself. I prefer fiction, drama that sort of thing. But I do recognise the name simply because you're the second person asking for it. Just this morning another young lady came in asking for the very same book. Let me see . . . yes, 'An Indian Adventure' by A. Srivastava. Well, the computer screen tells me we still have two copies in store. Would you like to follow me, the history books are kept at the far end.

After they purchased the book the girls decided to have lunch at a small sandwich bar round the corner. They were hungrily tucking into some bacon and Tomato baguettes when Abigail spotted someone familiar crossing the road.

"Psst," she nudged Elizabeth, "I think we've got company."

"Well, well, I didn't know her Royal Highness shopped like the rest of us. Didn't she mention she always goes abroad to do her shopping?"

Alison Radcliffe walked in. Her face went red when she saw Liz and Abi. She didn't want to be spotted in such a 'common' joint. She should never have listened to those idiots, Chloe and Michelle. It was their idea to come here in the first place. She could NOT let Elizabeth and Abigail see her eating in a place like this. Hmm, she'd have to think of something. Just then Chloe and Michelle walked in.

"Hey Chloe, I'm not feeling too good. I think it's the smell. I'm not used to such pungent odours. I'm going to that other restaurant near Ramsden Square. Are you two staying here or coming with me for some proper food?"

Alison made sure that her voice was soft enough not to disturb the other diners, but loud enough for Elizabeth and Abigail to notice. Since Alison was trying so hard to ignore them, Abi thought she'd better do the honours!

"Yoo-hoo, hello Alison, didn't you notice us? We were about to have some sandwiches. What about you?"

Abigail spoke at the top of her voice.

"No thank you. I was just waiting for Chloe and Michelle. We're actually having lunch at 'Cleo's', aren't we girls?"

"But," Chloe tried to resist but Alison pulled her away from the table.

"Come on you two. My legs are getting tired."

Alison picked up her bag and walked out of the cafe.

"Chloe wait. Elizabeth noticed that Alison had forgotten a shopping bag. She picked it up and ran after Chloe.

"Chloe I think Alison has forgotten this."

"Thanks Elizabeth, I'll give it to her."

When she handed the bag to Chloe, Elizabeth noticed that it was from 'A Few Words and More.' Oh! So Alison was shopping for books too. Liz wondered what sort of books Alison liked—paper backs, hard backs or more likely, 'Gold Rimmed'.

Abi and Liz were soon on their way back home.

"I need to get back to my maths, Abi. Mr Fletcher has given me two question papers to take in on Monday. It'll be my last lesson with him before the finals."

"Fine by me," said Abi, "got plenty to do myself. I can't believe how quickly the year's gone. So much has happened, yet it seems like only yesterday the school reopened after summer holidays."

"Yes," nodded Elizabeth. "So much has happened. More than I ever imagined." She smiled to herself thinking of her tiny friend waiting at home, probably tickling Toby with her wings.

"AAAArrrrrfffffffffff . . ."

"Whoa, that's a mighty sneeze from a dog, who ingested a lake-full of water some time ago."

Dr Atkins and Toby were going to the Vet for Toby's check up. "Bye Liz. Your mum's in the shower. Could you tell her I'll be back in an hour and don't forget to convey all of our best wishes to Ms Fitzgerald. She's one great teacher. Bye again, sweetheart . . ."

"Bye again sweetheart," a tiny voice mimicked Dr Atkins's.

"Huh, Tippy, where are you?"

Tippy was happily clinging on to Toby's collar.

"Oh, I see. Where do you think you're going?"

"I'm accompanying Toby. He needs my support when he meets the vet. Doctors can be *really tiresome* at times, can't they Dr Atkins!?"

"Tipeeeee!"

"Who are you kidding, Tippy," said Elizabeth, "we all know you'd say anything for a ride in the car"

Toby, Tippy and the *'tiresome'* doctor were soon on their way. Elizabeth set off for school. Today was Ms Fitzgerald's send off and there were going to be no lessons in the afternoon. There was a special school dinner planned.

When Elizabeth and Abigail got to school, Ms Fitzgerald was standing outside their classroom speaking to Alison.

"Thank you very much Alison. I will definitely be reading that very soon. Anything about India captivates me. It's such a rich country, its culture, tradition; simply fascinating. Thank you again. Gosh! You girls are going to spoil me."

Elizabeth looked at Abigail.

"'Anything about India', Abi, are you thinking what I'm thinking?!"

Abigail nodded.

"Yep, but I sure hope we're mistaken."

The girls reached the classroom just as Ms Fitzgerald placed the gift onto her desk. It was a book and the title was clearly visible—'An Indian Adventure'!

"Oh no!" whispered Elizabeth.

"The Little Weasel, she knew. She must have overheard us speaking in the library. Of all the rotten things to do, this is the limit. I could just strangle her." As usual, Abi was fuming.

"Hi there you two, is something wrong? You look startled."

Abigail gritted her teeth. Alison's smug expression combined with her *fake* air of concern was absolutely unbearable!

"Alison, don't pretend that you actually *do* care if something was wrong," she frowned. Had it not been for her upbringing and the constraints imposed by school etiquette, Abigail Swift would undoubtedly have punched Alison Radcliffe.

"Well, *I'm* extremely pleased. Ms Fitzgerald is absolutely delighted with the gift I gave her. It's a book about India. Apparently, India and gardening are her two passions."

Alison's gaze was unflinching, cold and arrogant accompanied by a smile which was equally unfeeling.

Liz and Abi stood dumbfounded. Surely Alison couldn't be this nasty.

"She *did* hear Liz. She quoted you word for word. How dare she do that?"

"Why not, Abi, Alison could have bought Ms Fitzgerald the same present even if she hadn't overheard us."

"Oh please, Liz, stop being so understanding. You know as well as I do, that Alison wouldn't know the difference between Indian History and the origin of wigwams. Come on, Liz. She's clever but not exactly the kind of person to go into a book shop looking for gifts! Not when there are a million and one department stores at her disposal"

Elizabeth sighed. "Well, what's done is done. The question is what I'm going to do about my gift. Ms Fitzgerald won't need two of the same books about India. Hmmm, it's almost time for lunch. I guess the only thing I can do is buy some chocolates from the school shop. They do stock some confectionary for the boarding students."

"I suppose you're right. But you'd better be quick. The whole school is going to be in the hall. You don't want to be missed. If anyone asks I'll just tell them you've gone to the loo."

Elizabeth hurriedly made her way to the adjoining building where the school shop was. She managed to find a box of Quality Street and some flowers. After she'd paid, Elizabeth made her way back to the dinner hall. Although she was trying hard not to, in her heart of hearts, Elizabeth felt extremely disappointed. Alison had stolen something very precious.

"I wish Tippy was here," she thought, "she always knows what to do. Oh well, probably sometimes nothing more *can* be done. Ms Fitzgerald, I sure hope you like chocolates . . ."

# An Unforgettable Farewell

THE GIRLS AT Primrose High waited in anticipation as Ms Barrymore made her way to the stage at the end of the hall.

"Good afternoon, everyone." she began. "I enjoyed that, how about all of you?"

Ms Barrymore's words were met with loud claps and cheering, the girls had definitely enjoyed their 'school dinner' today. No complaints whatsoever!

"As you all know, that delicious spread was in honour of a very special person."

Ms Barrymore smiled at Ms Fitzgerald who was seated along with some of the other teachers at the main table.

"Ms Fitzgerald arrived at this school 25 years ago. She was a newly qualified teacher, inexperienced and apprehensive yet clearly displaying the talent, determination and level headedness that has made her a beacon not only for you, but for every teacher fortunate enough to work with her."

Ms Barrymore's speech continued with some affectionate references to Ms Fitzgerald's early years as a member of staff. She also spoke of the recognition the school had attained through Ms Fitzgerald's work and her co operation with faculty members from other schools in the region.

Ms Barrymore handed the mike over to Louise Cunningham, the Head girl, who spoke on behalf of all the students at Primrose High, expressing their gratitude and admiration.

Then it was Ms Fitzgerald's turn to speak.

"Good afternoon."

Ms Fitzgerald's voice was loud and clear

"I wasn't sure how to begin. Who is my speech meant for? Should I address it to you all in turn—my colleagues, my Superiors, my subordinates, my students? No, that wouldn't be right. You see, when I thought about it, none of those terms describe who you are to me. You are actually much more. You're my family. I have spent as much time here in the past 25 years as I have at my own home. We have laughed together, cried together, celebrated our victories together and, together, learnt from our mistakes."

Although Ms Fitzgerald spoke unfalteringly, the emotion in her tone was evident.

"You know girls; you may think that we're the teachers. But I can assure you that I have learnt more from you than any book could ever teach me. Sharing your experiences on your journey through High school has made my life more colourful. Thanks to you, I know everything I need to know about a young girl's mind and heart.

When I joined school twenty five years ago, I was not only a newly qualified teacher; I was also a newly qualified 'wife'. When my husband and I were expecting our first child, I used to imagine myself as the perfect mother to my little daughter. Surely the time I spend with wonderful girls like you would give me enough 'expertise' to mould my own daughter into a confident young lady. As things turned out, I was blessed with two sons!"

There were claps and laughter as Ms Fitzgerald continued.

"Yes, they're both now strapping young men. One is eighteen and the other Twenty two. Yet, even after being their mother all these years, I'm afraid I still can't comprehend how the male psyche works. I'm planning to work on that once I retire."

Ms Fitzgerald continued her speech with anecdotes of some of the blunders she made when she first became a teacher. After thanking her colleagues and the rest of the staff for their support through the years, Ms Fitzgerald paused and took a deep breath. She looked around the hall at the students who loved and respected her so much. She spotted Elizabeth sitting next to Abigail and smiled.

"Finally, to my girls, my advice to you is simple. Let your *heart* decide where you want to go in life, but make sure you let your *head* decide which route you follow to get there. Thank you all. Thank you so very much."

Ms Fitzgerald received a standing ovation. There were hugs, claps and tears as students and teachers went on stage to give their favourite teacher an unforgettable farewell.

"Come in,"

Elizabeth opened the door. Ms Fitzgerald was sat at her desk looking through some of the cards the girls had given her.

"Oh, hello Liz, I must say I'm quite overwhelmed. Look at all these presents."

"You deserve it Ms Fitzgerald. You're the best."

"Thank you, dear. What can I do for you? Why don't you sit down?"

Liz pulled up a chair resting her bag beside Ms Fitzgerald's desk.

"The revision is going according to plan, Ms Fitzgerald. Mr Fletcher has helped tremendously."

"You're showing marked improvement, Elizabeth. Don't lose focus and you *will* succeed."

Elizabeth smiled and stood up with the bouquet.

"Thank you Ms Fitzgerald. Actually, I came to give you these."

Elizabeth held out the flowers. Ms Fitzgerald hugged Elizabeth, flowers and all.

"You are precious sweetheart. Thank you Liz, it's the perfect gift. I couldn't have asked for anything better."

"Oh you're most welcome Ms. If you have a vase I'll put them in some water for you"

Elizabeth looked around trying to spot a vase.

"Elizabeth, when I said 'perfect gift' I wasn't talking about the flowers, even though they are pretty."

Elizabeth looked at Ms Fitzgerald with a bewildered expression.

"I'm sorry Ms Fitzgerald. I don't understand."

"I'm talking about the book. What a wonderful, thoughtful idea."

"The *book, Ms* Fitzgerald?"

Elizabeth was thoroughly mystified now.

"Yes Liz, the book that's peeping out of your half open school bag. The book, that Alison Radcliffe so 'lovingly' presented to me this morning. Apparently, she'd had the idea all along! Ha!"

Elizabeth's puzzlement had turned to disbelief. How could Ms Fitzgerald possibly know?

"Don't look so surprised dear. Having my office next to the girls' locker room has many advantages."

"I can't believe this!"

"Well, it's true, Elizabeth. Liz, if it's not too much trouble would you let me keep the book. It would mean so much to me."

"I don't know what to say, Ms Fitzgerald. I mean, of course you can keep it. It would mean a lot to me too. But what would you do with two copies of the same book."

Ms Fitzgerald laughed.

"They're not the same Liz. One is from Alison and this one is from you. To me that makes a very big difference. You're special Elizabeth. I'm going to miss you."

"I'll miss you too, Ms Fitzgerald. I'll miss you lots." Elizabeth hugged her favourite teacher.

"Thank you Ms Fitzgerald. Thanks for everything."

"God bless you, Lizzie. Now run along and good luck for your exams."

Elizabeth was overjoyed. She couldn't wait to tell Abi. In fact, she'd better tell Abi soon, before Abi had the chance to cause serious bodily harm to Alison!!! She was already fed up with Alison Radcliffe and Alison's most recent self glorifying tactic was the last straw. The extent that the girl would go just to try and outshine everyone else was beyond words! Liz chuckled to herself at the thought of Abigail grabbing Alison by the collar and giving her a well deserved rattle.

# Exam Fever

FINAL EXAMS WERE in full swing at Primrose High. Elizabeth had only two more papers to go, History and Mathematics. She was happy with the ones she'd done.

"I think I'll pass, mum," said Elizabeth, gulping down some chicken soup.

"Excuse me. I hope you will more than just 'pass."

Elizabeth grinned. "I was kidding, mum. I'm sure I've done well. But the worst is yet to come. I'm not looking forward to tomorrow. I better go up straight after supper and revise the formulae once more."

Elizabeth knew she shouldn't be trying to cram on the eve of the exam But she could not afford to make any mistakes. She shouldn't. Not with all the help and encouragement she'd got. Not with Mr Fletcher's classes. No. She had to get things right. Liz could feel her heart pounding when she thought of the exam. What if it was tough? Formulae, formulae, formulae, Trigonometry, Pythagoras theorem, Gosh! She couldn't remember anything. Her mind was going blank.

"Oh, no!" Elizabeth exclaimed, with her hands clutching the sides of her head.

"Liz, come here sweetheart." Liz's mum had followed her upstairs with Tippy. She placed Liz's head onto her shoulder and gently stroked her brown hair. "Calm down, Lizzy. The last thing you want to do is work yourself up. You need to rest. Your *mind* needs a rest."

"Your mum is right, Lizzy. You must try and relax. You need to be calm and composed to perform well Liz," the little fairy was now perched on Liz's knee.

"Elizabeth, you have already put in a lot of effort these past few months and that's all that matters. That's all we want from you Lizzy, to try your best. Why don't you get ready for bed? That's enough number crunching for tonight."

Elizabeth had no choice but to listen. Actually, she didn't mind. Its only when she lay down that she realised just how exhausted she was.

"I love you mummy."

"I love you too, Sweetie pie'"

"Hey, what about me?"

Tippy was fluttering round in circles.

"Ok ok, we love you too, Tippy. Now let's go down and clear up. Helena's probably fallen asleep on the sofa, conveniently avoiding any kitchen work!

Tippy looked at Elizabeth, already half asleep under her duvet.

"I hope she does well, Mrs Atkins,"

"So do I, Tippy, So do I."

Elizabeth twitched her nose uncomfortably. Something was crawling onto her face. Oh no. It can't be that earth worm that Helena found in the garden. Eeeeeaaaaou!!!She jumped up screaming. Eyes wide open.

"Hey, it's just me silly. I've been trying to wake you up for the past five minutes and you wouldn't budge. So I tiptoed over your nose."

"Tipee! What time is it? Why did you wake me up when there's no school."

"Get up sleeping beauty, its results day. Anyway, aren't you glad you woke up? The way you just screamed you must have been in the middle of a nightmare. Hmmm . . . can you call it a 'night' mare, when it's actually morning? In any case, 'nightmare' or 'morning mare' thanks to me it won't disturb you anymore."

Elizabeth rubbed her eyes. She looked at Tippy and frowned. Why did she have to wake up, that too, for the horrible results?

"You're wrong little miss killjoy. Your tiny toes tiptoeing over my face woke me up! The thought of looking at the results board is the nightmare. Oh well, It can't be avoided. Who knows, I might get an A+ in Maths!! Imagine that, me getting an A+ in maths. Like I told Ms Roberts, pigs would have to fly before that happens!"

"Pigs fly? Unbelievable isn't it. Elizabeth, look at me. Do you remember that day, almost a year ago? If I'm not mistaken, something quite unbelievable happened to you—ME. A real fairy! How preposterous, yet, how true! I'm here aren't I? So, my darling Elizabeth, do NOT underestimate pigs. One day, they may just fly! More importantly, do not underestimate yourself. One day, you may get an A+ in Maths.

Besides, like your mum told you, the result does matter but not as much as your determination and effort. It's not about reaching the summit, Liz. It's about enjoying the climb. Learning new things, overcoming obstacles, picking yourself up when you slip—and there *will* be times when you slip. In those moments, your greatest strength won't be your Maths grade; it'll be your motivation to never give up."

Elizabeth was staring at Tippy as though she had spoken in a foreign language, a blank expression which suggested that either she wasn't paying any attention to Tippy's Words of Wisdom or she hadn't understood them.

"Elizabeth! Are you still asleep?!"

"No Tippy. I am not. I appreciate every word you just said but I'm desperate for the toilet!"

With sudden urgency, Liz got out of bed. As she reached the bathroom, she turned and looked at Tippy.

"I really do understand what you said, Tippy. But right now my nerves are way beyond listening to anyone or anything."

"Don't worry, Liz. You'll be ok. See you downstairs." Tippy fluttered off. Downstairs Dr Atkins was reading the weekend newspaper. "Come on Liz, why the long face? Don't look so worried."

"I can't help it Dad," said Elizabeth sitting down next to her father. "I just want to get it over with."

"But the exams *are* over."

"Not the exams, Dad, the results."

"Oh, those, when were you in charge of the results?!"

"Dad! Mum, why is Dad being so difficult, he knows what I mean."

Liz's mother looked at Dr Atkins and smiled.

"Come on Richard, she's nervous enough already."

"Christine, I am just trying to make her lighten up. Listen darling, whatever the result, it is ok. You have done your bit. Now cheer up because we are all going out this evening to celebrate."

"Celebrate!! Celebrate what? Dad, I don't know the results yet."

"That's my point, it doesn't matter. We're going any way."

"Wow . . . Dr Atkins . . . did you hear that Liz? *You're going anyway.* Your Dad is kind of cool after all!" Tippy started doing some sort of a jig on the dining table. Her tiny feet brushed against Dr Atkins's open newspaper.

"What do you mean 'kind of cool', Tippy? There is no one cooler. The word was coined after me."

"Yeah, of course it was Dad," said Elizabeth rolling her eyes. "I better get going." Elizabeth took a deep breath. She hugged her parents. "I'm so nervous, mum."

Christine Atkins kissed Elizabeth, "Good Luck, sweetheart."

Elizabeth put the phone down and fastened her coat.

"Toby, not now, I want to go, Toby. Please get out of the way." Bartholomew had suddenly decided that he should reaffirm his affection and loyalty to Elizabeth and was strategically positioned in front of the door. He clambered on to Elizabeth and slobbered her with licks as she tried in vain to inch forward.

"Toby, move now" Liz yelled. "What's wrong with you?"

Toby immediately quietened down. Elizabeth never shouted at him. How *could* she. She of all people! This was not acceptable. He was hurt. Fine, if Elizabeth wanted him to move he would move. And that was that. A picture of remorse and self pity, Bartholomew Atkins flopped down determined not to move a muscle. Why should he bother, nobody cared. He would add a few tear jerking whimpers just for effect. That should do the trick. Liz is bound to regret her actions.

Just then something prodded Toby's well padded belly. "Toby, I need to open the door. Oh mum! He has plonked himself in front of the door now."

Dr Atkins put his coffee cup down. "Bartholomew, get out of the way, boy." The stern tone had immediate effect. Toby repositioned himself behind the sofa.

"Aah ... now I feel sorry for him. You shouldn't have shouted at him, Dad. Toby, come here."

"Elizabeth, excuse me! What do you mean I shouldn't have shouted at him? You are the one who wanted me to get Toby out of the way."

"I second that Liz, you're being difficult." Tippy was tickling Toby's ears with her wings. "If you're feeling that so sorry for him, take him with you, he needs a good walk anyway."

"Huh? now? Mum!" Elizabeth looked up at her mum for some support. She was tense about the results and she couldn't be bothered with Toby's tantrums. But Mrs Atkins didn't offer any solutions. "I think it is a wonderful idea. He'll keep you distracted. You won't be able to ponder over your marks too much. Tippy you'll go too, won't you?"

"Of course, I will. I was going to accompany Liz anyway. Come on Toby, let's go for a good long walk. I mean you can walk, I'll just enjoy the ride."

Elizabeth's mum was right. The minute they left The Kowhai, Toby's engines were in full throttle. "Gosh Toby, I didn't think you still had it in you," panted Liz. "Phew, I am exhausted."

They had arrived at the school gates. There were some cars in the staff car park. Summer holidays had started but the staff had one more week before the term ended. Elizabeth made her way to the main office. The results were posted on the notice board. Liz could feel her heart thumping.

"Tippy will you have a look for me, please. I don't want to be disappointed."

"What difference is it going to make, silly. Your results are your results, whether you look or I look."

"Please Tippy, Please . . . I know it doesn't make any sense but please . . .".

They stood in front of the notice board. Elizabeth purposely avoided looking at the list.

"Did you find it? How did I do?"

"Well, I think you did ok. Four A's, four A+'s and a B +." Tippy noticed the disappointment on Liz's face.

"Hello, I think four A's and four A+'s deserve a smile at least. Why do you look as though you've failed?"

"Oh, do I? Yes, I know I should be happy. It's just that deep down I was hoping for an A in Maths. I know I shouldn't be asking for too much. I mean a B Plus is good considering I only ever got a B. Sorry Tippy, for sounding so . . ."

"Stop blabbering for a moment, Liz. Who said you got the B+ in Maths. Elizabeth, could you *please look at the notice board*! You've got an A in Maths."

Elizabeth's head was reeling. Disappointment had turned into incredulity. An A in Maths! It was a dream.

"Hello, Elizabeth, lovely day isn't it?" Elizabeth turned round to see Ms Bannister and Ms Roberts.

"Good morning, Ms Bannister. Yes, it is a nice day," Elizabeth looked puzzled. Although it was summer, the sky outside was overcast.

"Don't look so confused dear; I was not referring to the weather." Ms Bannister eyed the notice board. "We are proud of you, Liz. This goes to show that there is nothing a determined mind can't achieve. Well done."

Ms Roberts congratulated Elizabeth as well.

"Great work, Liz. Oh! I was just going to tell Ms Bannister that we need to keep an eye on the sky today. If it clears up, we might just be able to spot a few pigs up there!"

Elizabeth laughed.

"Nothing's impossible Elizabeth," Ms Roberts pointed to the notice board, "your grades prove it."

Thrilled beyond words, Elizabeth was soon on her way back home. Toby had used up so much of his energy on the outbound journey that Elizabeth had to keep prodding him to speed up. Now *she* was the one in a hurry.

The sky was no longer a dismal grey. With the summer sunshine peeping through the clouds, Elizabeth trekked up the hills towards the Kowhai. She stopped by the little stream, where almost a year ago, she had heard a little voice. The little voice spoke to her again. "See I told you it's not that bad."

"Tippy," said Elizabeth holding Tippy's little hand in hers as she sat down next to the stream, "please don't go. All of a sudden I am scared. Since my maths has improved, I'm afraid that you'll leave me, that you will disappear as suddenly as you came."

Tippy kissed Elizabeth. "My dear sweet Elizabeth, do you actually think that I came all the way here to help you with your Maths? Good grief no! You have got far more serious issues. For starters, you talk too much! Now stop getting all sentimental and get a move on. I've got a handsome Doctor friend waiting to escort me to dinner."

Toby, who was enjoying his leisurely walk home, suddenly jolted into action, when Tippy tickled his nostrils with a blade of grass. Soft squeals of excitement amidst clouds of fairy dust added lustre to the warm summer breeze as Tippy fluttered her wings in frantic attempts to fend off Toby's gigantic paws.

What a year it had been. Serendipity was right. Things weren't that bad, they weren't that bad at all. In fact, they were magical.

"Hey, wait for me", Liz called after her companions.

Birds chirped gleefully. Butterflies thronged the fields surrounding The Kowhai and the yellow buttercups lent a golden radiance to the sun-bathed hills. Nature's song was *almost* as sweet as Elizabeth's fairy tale . . .

## A FEW YEARS LATER ...

Lizzy, that was Jonathan. He said he'll be here in half an hour. Elizabeth, can you hear me? God, she's seventeen and still probably day dreaming. Lizzy ..."

Elizabeth's mum started making her way up to Elizabeth's bedroom when, someone suddenly crept up from behind making her jump.

"Boo!!"

"Elizabeth!!"

"Mum, didn't you notice me come down earlier. I needed to borrow your Mascara. By the way, mum, I heard what you said. I am not 'seventeen and daydreaming', so there!"

"Of course you're not, I can see that. You're more like a seven year old, since you still seem to get so much delight from saying 'boo'. Oh! you look lovely Liz."

Elizabeth was wearing a full length olive green gown, her favourite evening dress. Her hair fell loosely over her shoulders with a single clip to hold her fringe in place. At seventeen, Mrs Atkins didn't have to be after Elizabeth to keep her hair tidy!

"Aren't you going to put your necklace on?"

Mrs Atkins waited for a reply from Elizabeth.

"Lizzy, what are you looking for? Didn't you hear me?

"Elizabeth's eyes were darting all round the room, searching.

"Where is she, Mum? Is she hiding to surprise me? Come on Tippy. I've waited long enough. Game's over. Come on out."

"Lizzy, Tippy isn't here, honest. We haven't seen her, sweetheart."

The smile vanished from Elizabeth's face.

"She isn't? No. That can't be. Tippy has to be here somewhere. Maybe she's hiding from all of us. She wouldn't miss today."

"Elizabeth, calm down. Jonathan will be here in a few minutes. Why don't you go and finish getting dressed. Don't worry about Tippy. Who knows, she might jump out of the salad bowl at dinner."

Upstairs, Elizabeth glanced at her reflection in the full length mirror. As she tried to fasten her necklace, she smiled to herself. In a couple of months, she would be in University, doing what she'd always dreamed of doing, a degree in Fine Arts. Her high grades had even won her a scholarship. It felt wonderful, but something was missing, someone was missing. Elizabeth continued to fumble with her necklace.

"My, my, who's this? Miss World?"

Elizabeth jumped and the necklace fell.

"Oops . . . hope it isn't broken."

Elizabeth couldn't believe it.

"Tippeeee! You're back! I thought you wouldn't come back this time."

There she was—as tiny, as beautiful and as magical as ever. Serendipity was sat on the edge of Liz's bedside locker, one fairy leg gracefully placed over the other.

"Don't be silly. I wouldn't miss today for the world"

Elizabeth sat down on her bed and gently squeezed Tippy's feathery fingers.

"I missed you Tippy. I know you've gone home before, but never for this long. I was beginning to worry that maybe . . ."

Elizabeth stopped speaking as if afraid to complete the sentence.

"That maybe I'd never come back?"

Elizabeth nodded.

"Yes, kind of . . . I guess."

"Lizzy, Lizzy, Lizzy. Hmmm, we'll talk about that later. First, there's someone I'd like you to meet."

Elizabeth's mouth fell open when she saw the person Serendipity had bought with her. From behind the lampshade on the corner of the bedside locker, a creature the size of a grape made its way towards Tippy. On closer scrutiny, Elizabeth saw that it looked exactly like a dog, a miniature poodle with wings.

"Liz, this is Diddy. I wanted you to meet him. Rather I wanted him to meet you. After all, you're the reason why Diddy and I are such good friends now."

When Elizabeth tried to touch Diddy, he crouched down behind Tippy.

"Amazing!!!!! He's so cute, Tippy. Will Diddy be staying with us too?"

Just then there was a knock at the door.

"It's me Liz"

The voice brought a shy smile to Elizabeth's face.

"Who is it Lizzy?" asked Tippy curiously.

Elizabeth put a finger to her lips.

"Shush. He's a friend of mine. Hide somewhere for a second."

Liz opened the door to a smartly attired young man with brown wavy hair and glasses.

"Wow, you look great. Shall we make a move?"

"Actually Jonathan, could you give me five more minutes. There's something I need to do for Helena before we leave. I'll join you downstairs."

"That's fine Liz."

Jonathan turned to go and then stopped. His head tilted towards Elizabeth and he planted a quick kiss on her cheek.

"Don't be too long."

Elizabeth closed the door after him and went back to the dresser.

Cheeky as ever, Serendipity was quick to pounce.

"Oooooh, what a 'friendly' friend you have my dear. I always knew you'd go for the 'nerdy' type." Elizabeth blushed but was quick to retaliate.

"What! First of all, what do you mean by 'go for'? Jonathan is a wonderful, considerate person and a good friend. And when I say 'friend' I mean exactly that, 'a friend', nothing more, nothing less. Secondly, just because he wears glasses it doesn't mean he's a nerd. Gosh Tippy! I thought you were above all this silly teasing. I mean, the moment you become a teenager, people make mountains out of molehills every time you speak to a boy. How childish!"

"Well, I'm not the one getting all hot and bothered. So you tell me who's being childish?"

Elizabeth gave up.

"Fine, you win. So is Diddy going to be staying with us too? That would be great."

"Actually Lizzy, Diddy won't be staying. He has to go back. I have to go back too because . . ."

"Go back, now? Hope everything is alright. Aren't your parents ok. But you just came. Will you be gone for long?"

"Slow down, Elizabeth, let me complete what I was going to say. My parents are fine. Everything is OK. When I said I'm going home I mean I won't be coming back. Liz, I have to go."

Elizabeth looked at Tippy and let out a nervous giggle.

"Very nice, fairy God Mother, this isn't the time for jokes Tippy. I better go down now. I'll see you after the Prom. Can't wait to tell you about what happened to Alison Radcliffe on the last day."

"Elizabeth. I'm not joking. This is it Liz. You always knew I'd leave you one day. Today is the day. I came back to say thank you Liz. Thank you for being such a great mate."

"Tippy", Elizabeth sat down on the floor holding Tippy in the palm of her hand, "you're serious aren't you? But you can't go. What would I do without you? Tippy, please. I don't understand. I mean you said everyone was ok at home. So, what's the rush? And Diddy can stay too. I'm sure we can find another shoe box for him."

Elizabeth was in tears. She couldn't believe it.

"Please Tippy. I've done so many things, achieved so much all because of you and your magic. What will I do now?"

"Shush, quieten down, Liz. Now listen to me carefully. You're right. You've achieved a lot. But in all these years what you didn't realise is that I had nothing to do with it. You did. I didn't give you any easy answers, Liz. You found them yourself. I never fought your battles Liz. You did. Remember you were so afraid of how you would cope without Toby. Yet when we lost him you found the strength to console *me*. You can do anything you want Elizabeth. The magic is within you. I had nothing to do with it."

Elizabeth wiped her face sniffing as she gulped down more tears

"You've got so much going for you Liz—new adventures, new challenges, and new *relationships*," Serendipity eyed the door and winked at Elizabeth.

"I must leave now Lizzy, so that you start believing in your own magic—not mine." Tippy kissed Elizabeth.

"Goodbye Liz. I'll always love you."

There was a sudden cloud of fairy dust and Serendipity was gone.

Mrs Atkins opened Liz'z bedroom door to find her sobbing.

"What's wrong Liz. Jonathan's been waiting quite a while sweetheart. What is it Lizzy? Are you hurt?"

"She's gone mum. Tippy's gone forever."

Elizabeth held on to her mother and cried.

Downstairs Jonathan Ashcroft looked at the clock on the mantelpiece. The prom would have started. He adjusted his bowtie and glanced upstairs. Jonathan sighed and sat back on the sofa. What's half an hour in a lifetime? He'd wait. He'd wait for as long as it would take. Elizabeth Atkins was worth it.

Outside, a starlit sky complemented the aura of a full moon looming proudly over the hills. In the shrubbery beneath the Kowhai's large bay window, a family of fireflies watched curiously as a peculiar creature flew down next to them. Although it was twice their size the fireflies weren't frightened and they moved closer. This new 'insect' didn't seem very interested in them.

Tiny silver droplets which shone in the fireflies' luminescence were streaming down its face.

Somewhere in the skies a bird flapped its wings as it made its way home. The moon smiled at them—all of nature's creations, the big, the small and the miraculous!

MANY YEARS LATER ...

"THANK YOU, PROF Brown. I'll have the papers sent to you by Monday."

Elizabeth put down the receiver and rearranged some of the folders spread out on her table.

"Jonathan, could you put the kettle on, please. I'd love a cup of coffee."

"Liz, shouldn't Emily be home now? It's already quarter past four."

Elizabeth looked at her husband and shook her head, smiling. He'd been pacing up and down for more than fifteen minutes, looking at the time every now and then.

"They're only meant to be back by five, at the earliest. Jonathan stop being so paranoid. It's only a school trip, for God's sake. At this rate what are you going to be like when Emily starts going out with her friends?"

Liz was about to pour some milk into her coffee when the doorbell rang.

"Aaah, that must be Daddy's precious princess!" Elizabeth teased.

Jonathan eagerly opened the door.

"Hello sweetheart. Did you have a good time?"

With long brown hair, Emily looked a lot like Elizabeth except for her dimpled smile which she'd inherited from her dad.

"Hey, where's my favourite smile? Are you all right, Emily?"

Elizabeth was at the door now with her coffee.

"Don't just stand there sweetie, come in. Emily, why do you look so perplexed. What is it? Didn't you have a good time?"

Emily looked up at her mother.

"You won't believe who I met today, mummy. I've made a new friend, a very special friend . . ."

# From My Heart ...

'Serendipity' is my modest endeavour to try and capture the imagination of a few tiny minds. I do have a secret hope that one day it will line the shelves of book stores all over the world, but that's my secret. Nobody need know. What I would like everyone to know, is that I owe this story to some special people who enrich my life and share my dreams—my friends and my family. I express my sincere gratitude for their love, motivation and support all these years.

Thank you.
Rashmi Kaimal

RASHMI KAIMAL WAS born in 1976 in Kerala, South India. She holds a Bachelors Degree in International Tourism and a MSc in Quality Management. She currently resides in the UK with her husband and two daughters.

'Serendipity's emphasis on encouraging creativity is reflective of Rashmi's own love of Art in any form. Having trained in Indian Classical Dance and Music for a number of years, she feels that there is nothing more enriching for children than being given the opportunity to discover, explore and develop their own interests and talents.

So, how is it that a 'thirty plus' mother of two—someone who once obtained fairly decent marks in Mathematics and Science, someone who is considered of sound and stable mind by all those who know her—chose to write a story about something as implausible as a fairy? Rashmi's answer is this:

Rashmi does not believe in fairy tales, however, she does believe that we tread a fine line between dreams and reality. She believes that with the right encouragement and determination dreams can come true. As far as the 'implausibility' goes, well, aren't children proof enough that miracles do happen.

Printed in Great Britain
by Amazon